I adjusted my weight from one leg to the other. "So," I began. "Are you going to the Spring Carnival next Friday?"

Brett stared at me for a second, almost like he didn't know what I meant.

"You know, Spring Carnival?"

He smiled again. And oh, was his smile distracting. "Yeah. I'll be there. Why?"

Why? I hadn't thought that far.

"Oh, nothing. I'm just, my friends and I. We have a booth. I think, I mean maybe you've seen our Facebook page. It's just this, like —"

"The kissing booth? I know." He breathed in and out slowly. "So you'll be working at the kissing booth? At the fair?"

By now I could feel my ears burning again. "Well, sort of. I mean yeah." I tried to shrug, like it wasn't a big deal — like it wasn't the *biggest deal ever.*

Kissing Booth

✦ LEXIE HILL ✦

No part of this work may be reproduced, stored in a retrieval system, or transmitted in any form or by any means, electronic, mechanical, photocopying, recording, or otherwise, without written permission of the publisher. For information regarding permission, write to Scholastic Inc., Attention: Permissions Department, 557 Broadway, New York, NY 10012.

ISBN-13: 978-0-545-07865-8
ISBN-10: 0-545-07865-2

Copyright © 2009 by Lexie Hill
All rights reserved. Published by Scholastic Inc.

SCHOLASTIC, POINT, and associated logos are trademarks and/or registered trademarks of Scholastic Inc.

Trademarks used herein are owned by their respective trademark owners and are used without permission.

Library of Congress Cataloging-in-Publication Data Available

12 11 10 9 8 7 6 5 4 3 2 1   9 10 11 12 13 14/0

Printed in the U.S.A.
First printing, January 2009
Text design by Steve Scott

With thanks to Aimee, Morgan, and Abby

Kissing Booth

Chapter 1

Sunday, 6p.m.

"So how was he?" I asked, trying to pin back my dark hair before it went completely limp again.

Note to self: Never try to cut my own hair. It had finally grown back to shoulder length after I went nuts on it a couple months ago and chopped it all off. It was all the fault of Sun-In, which had turned my hair orange, and I just couldn't wait for it to grow out.

Other note to self: Never dye.

"Robbie F?" Bella scoffed, whipping her mini-hairbrush out of her huge shoulder bag, which was lying on my bed next to Bella herself.

"Yeah, I mean, was he a good kisser or what?" I spread on my strawberry "extra-smoochable" lip gloss. It feels like glue, which seems counterintuitive, right? But it's nice and shiny. "You are the queen of kiss-and-tell.

Don't make me drag it out of you," I added, grinning at her over my shoulder.

Bella swung her Diesel-jeaned legs off of the dorky old Pooh Bear pillow I keep on my bed. "Ugh, please don't remind me. Lisi, he wears *braces* and we were at the *movies*, so his mouth was full of popcorn." Bella shuddered.

"That's why you broke up with him?" Bella dates a guy a minute practically.

She chose to ignore my question, though, instead leaping up and nudging me to the side. "Come on, NBK, scooch over and let me use the mirror for a sec!"

"Stop calling me that!" I nudged her back.

"Well, you ARE, aren't you? Meanwhile, some of us have actual intentions of making out in the near future and need to *prepare*." Bella smirked at me as she began her manic hair-brushing routine.

NBK. I truly hate it when she calls me that. But she's right. It's true. Never Been Kissed. That's me.

Bella and I are sixteen. We are getting our driver's licenses this summer. We are juniors in high school. We are totally normal. *I* am totally normal. Except for one little detail. The NBK status.

All my friends have kissed people. Bella's kissed, like, well, I think seven or eight guys that I know of, but there were probably more. And my other best friend, Mo, kissed that boy at camp two summers in a row, and then kissed Ryan Peabody behind the bleachers which was *such* a cliché but at least she can say she's kissed people. As for Johnny, my guy best friend (and the only one of us who already has his license), he kissed this freshman girl Sandra last year who ended up moving to Kentucky, and I love telling him that she had to leave the state after experiencing The Johnny. He gets uber-red whenever we tease him about girls — so of course we do it as much as possible.

As for me, I guess you could say I'm picky. That's part of it. Then of course there is The Curse. In second grade, a boy named Danny confessed his love for me in front of the whole classroom during snack time. He leaned in to kiss me — at least, I assume that's what he was trying to do — but I was so mortified I choked on my banana and ran away coughing and screaming "Ew!" I didn't intend to be mean or anything. But that incident has always haunted me, like maybe I jinxed myself by refusing the one guy who actually said "I love you." Never mind that we were seven at the time. It could still be bad karma.

But even worse than The Curse is, well, The Crush.

And by *Crush* I mean "total and complete life-altering obsession." I am convinced that my silent, well-hidden crush on Brett Jacobson, one of the most popular seniors in my school, has permanently stunted my social development and prevented me from ever finding the right opportunity to get kissed. It's not like I don't *want* to. I *definitely* want to kiss someone.

It's just that I want my first kiss to be with Brett Jacobson. But the problem is, Brett is completely and utterly out of my league. Like, me guppy, him shark.

I rolled my eyes at Bella in the mirror before plopping down on my — now rumpled, thanks to her — cream-colored comforter. I watched her brush her long, straight, dirty-blond hair. Bella always looks like she just stepped out of a salon. Tonight she wore a tight black turtleneck and big gold earrings — pretty sophisticated for a Sunday.

I, on the other hand, was wearing a thin gray hoodie, jeans, and flip-flops. I picked up Pooh and smoothed his wrinkled red T-shirt, while Bella went on about her plans to snag some new boy. There was always some new boy.

It was officially the end of spring break. School was starting again tomorrow morning. But it was a Northside High tradition to grab a slice at Vinnie's on the last night of break, gossip about the upcoming Spring Carnival, and people-watch. Which is what Bella and I were getting ready to do. Everyone usually came back from cruises and Florida vacations way more tan than any self-respecting citizen of the Sucker State (aka the lovely Illinois) should have. We only live, like, thirty minutes outside of Chicago but Northside is *total* suburbia. At least that's what my sister, Claire, likes to say. She's in college now.

I kind of like Northside, though. It's a nice town, not too big. I grew up here. All my friends are here.

Mo is my oldest friend. Her real name is Molly Dean. Our moms went to college together a zillion years ago, but the first time we really became friends was in the sandbox in preschool. This mean kid named Jeremy Slack threw sand in my eyes, and I had to clench them shut. Mo was the one who took my hand and led me back inside to the bathroom and helped me wash my face. By the time the teacher got there, Mo had taken care of me. Even though we were only four and neither of us could even reach the paper towel dispenser in the bathroom! Mo had always been like that: totally reliable.

Bella is the opposite. She moved here with her mom in fifth grade when her parents got divorced. Back then, Bella had been kind of chubby, but she has since become a total slave to salads and seltzer to combat her curves, even though I am pretty sure it's her "curves" — two curves in particular — that get her so much attention from boys. And if there's anything Bella seems to like more than salads and seltzers, it's attention from boys. She inhales it like I would inhale a Slurpee™ from the 7-Eleven™, like it's the best thing she's ever tasted.

Bella only refers to her mother by her first name, Lucy. That's just the kind of person Bella is: confident, and she likes to do things her own way. Like now, for instance. She had finished brushing her hair and was raiding my closet without asking.

"Helloooo, Earth to Lisi!" she said.

"What?"

"I asked if you think I would look cute in little side ponytails?" Bella held her hair on either side of her face and grinned.

"Hey, lay off the 'do. *I* am all about the side ponytails!" I cried, sitting bolt upright. I love Bella, but I really hate it when she tries to copy something I do. I don't know why. I guess it's just that if it looked better on her, then I'd totally have to stop doing it. Because I really hate to compete.

"Uh-oh, don't mess with the girl's pony!" Bella laughed, galloping around my bedroom. That's the thing about Bella — in public she is like Mistress of Seduction, but behind closed doors she is a total nutcase.

"Hey, stop horsing around — get it? Horsing? But seriously, you're stepping on my clothes!" I couldn't help giggling a little. It can be pretty hard to stay annoyed with Bella.

"Neeheeheehee!" Bella screeched in some kind of warped impression of a pony, grabbing one of my socks from the carpeted floor and chucking it at my head.

"Are you neighing? Who *does* that?" I laughed, trying to pick up some of the clothes that were strewn everywhere now.

"I do," Bella replied. Every time she does something crazy and Bella-ish, I always say *who does that*? or *who says that*? and Bella answers *I do*. It's our thing.

"So," she went on. "Is it okay if I borrow these?" She held up a pair of lime-green sandals with high heels that I'd actually stolen from Claire's room. "I need to be tall for Mason," she said, pleadingly.

"Mason?"

"Duh, he's the BT!" *BT* meant "Boy Target," meaning the latest guy Bella was after.

"Mason Firestone?"

"Why not? Do you think he's too good for me or something?" Bella demanded, the green heels dangling from her fingers like weird tentacles.

"No, of course not! It's just . . ." I trailed off. It's just that Mason Firestone was captain of varsity baseball, a senior, and most importantly, best friends with Brett Jacobson.

"You don't think he'll be at Vinnie's?" she asked.

I looked away, suddenly feeling like I was going to burst into a million pieces — a feeling that had become more and more familiar all year. I began chipping at the collage of magazine pictures I'd taped on my pale blue wall over the desk. It was right next to a photo of me, Mo, and Bella at the eighth-grade formal. We'd all worn different shades of pink dresses because, when you're in middle school, stuff like that seems hilarious. Mo looked like a little angel in hers, with her blond curls tied back. Bella was wearing something magenta and way too tight (that was before she lost the baby fat), and I had my hair in one of those cheesy buns where they leave a strand hanging down. We all look super happy in that picture. It's just so *eighth grade*; that's why I love it.

But now I felt a horrible pang in my stomach. Note to self: Never, ever keep a major secret from one of my best friends again.

Johnny had no idea either. The only friend who knew about my epic, three-year crush on Brett was Mo. And of course Claire, but she was at Oberlin, almost four hundred miles away.

I'd told Mo because I *knew* she'd never ever break a promise and tell anyone. Bella, on the other hand, was a different breed. She always had the best intentions but . . . how could I have told her that I, Lisi Jared, totally random NHS junior, was obsessed with one of the most popular boys in school, someone who didn't know my name, whom I'd never *actually* spoken to, and who happened to already have a girlfriend, the flawless Jacqueline Winslow?

Brett is one of those overachiever types who gets involved with everything. But not annoyingly so. He has friends on Stu Co, he hangs with the baseball guys, and even the hot tenors from choir. More impressively, Brett is now a full editor for *Northside Outlook*, our school paper, and is always printing these hilarious, biting commentaries about politics. *Politics!* Total genius. He's also on varsity tennis, and his tan, muscular-but-lean arms look amazing in his crisp white polo shirts whenever I just *happen* to pass by the courts on my way to chem lab. And need I mention his pale blue eyes that seem to comprehend what no one else sees?

I sighed and flattened down the piece of tape that was showing at the corner of the collage. For a minute I thought I'd just blurt everything out to Bella now, rip it off like a Band-Aid, get my mortification over with.

But then I thought, *We still have over a month of school left before Brett will graduate and leave forever.* Why make a big embarrassing mess and ruin everything now?

I sneaked a peak at Bella, who was still rummaging through my stuff. I'd held off telling her how I felt about Brett for nearly three whole years. As painful as it was to think that she had no idea, I could hold off a bit longer.

Because the thing about secrets is, the longer you keep one, the harder it is to tell.

Chapter 2

Sunday, 6:45p.m.

Triple car horn. Johnny.

"Come on, sad puppy. It's time for some thin crust." Luckily Bella makes exceptions to her salad and seltzer diet when it comes to Vinnie's. She swung her bag over her shoulder, grabbed my hand, and yanked me out of my bedroom and into the upstairs hall. We raced down the stairs.

"Mom, we're going to the square!" I called as we dashed out the door.

"Call by ten, sweetie." My mom's voice filtered out from the studio. She would probably be up half the night working on one of her nature paintings. I had seen her doing a lot of preliminary sketches when we were in Virginia visiting my grandparents over break, and I sensed she was about to get into one of her "zones."

She could be in the studio for days and not even change her clothes.

Meanwhile, my dad was still at his office in Chicago. On a Sunday night. He's an advertising executive and almost never home. The best thing about having two parents who are both so obsessed with their own careers is that they don't spend a lot of time worrying about my life. They are pretty relaxed when it comes to rules, and I don't even have a curfew.

Now if only I had a reason to break a curfew in the first place. . . .

"Bye, Mrs. Jared," Bella sang as we dashed out the front door. We hopped down the front steps and ran to Johnny's car.

It used to be his dad's car, and it has this very Rothberg family smell that I kind of find comforting. Before Johnny used to give us rides, his dad would carpool all of us to school, so I've been riding in it since I was, like, nine. The reason Johnny and I got to be friends way back then was because we were tied as the fourth-grade math champions (dorky, I know). He and Mo and I quickly became a unit, and then when Bella moved to town, she joined our group. So in some ways I am like the nexus of our friend group. But it doesn't always feel like that.

"Dude, you're, like, twenty minutes late," Bella stated, strapping into the front seat and rolling down the window.

Johnny swiveled around to smile my way. He'd grown a lot taller in the last year, to the point where his dark, semi-curly hair touched the roof of the car.

I smiled, too, leaning against the backseat and breathing in the fresh air. I let my (not too shamefully) tanned arm rest out the car window. It was spring, and Northside was beginning to stay warm in the evenings. It was close to the end of the year, close to summer, and it felt like a time for possibilities. New beginnings. Fresh starts.

"We are so not going to get a seat at Vinnie's. Lisi and I are like starving children from Ethiopia," Bella went on.

I caught Johnny's dark eyes in the rearview mirror and could tell he was trying not to laugh at Bella.

"Sorry, ladies," he answered in his "important" voice. "I was just editing this *very* revealing cut of that new girls' basketball coach, Ms. Lewis, talking to Mr. Lory in the hall. I smell a *luuve* affair in the making."

Johnny was referring to this "mockumentary" of our school, which he'd been laboring over since September. He is the biggest film geek, and he'd been carrying his handheld digital camera *everywhere*. It's crazy. He's planning to submit the mockumentary to the Tisch School of the Arts in New York City as his application sample.

"My material was really lacking that extra level of parallel social discourse," Johnny added.

"Parallel what?" Bella asked.

"It's a thing I'm noticing about Martinez — he uses the interactions of side characters to illuminate the tension between the main players. Mr. Lory and Ms. Lewis are key side characters," Johnny explained.

Lately, Johnny had been referencing Martinez a lot. According to Johnny, Luc Martinez was a visionary young filmmaker. All I knew was that Luc Martinez was a superhot Diego Luna look-alike who acted as well as directed. Mr. Lory, on the other hand — not so steamy.

"Yuck." I wrinkled my nose. "Mr. Lory is, like, over forty."

"Yeah, but he's kinda hot, in a someone-else's-dad way," Bella said.

"A dad way?" I shouted, leaning forward so my head was in between the two front seats. "Gross. Who even says that?"

"I do!"

Johnny laughed and then shouted "Score!" as he whipped the car into a rare free parking spot behind the restaurant.

The three of us slid into a sticky faux leather booth at Vinnie's. It was one of only two left. Even though the place was pretty big, we were right up front by the windows, the least cool part of the restaurant. The Populars always dominated the back booths. I sat down facing the window since I knew Bella was all about facing the inside and scoping everyone out. I didn't mind looking out at the view of the sun setting instead. Plus, I was keeping a lookout for Mo.

Johnny sat next to me. He smelled kind of like his car but mixed with boys' deodorant. To me, that is the scent of sanity.

"So," Bella said, after we'd ordered a large Hawaiian thin crust, "speaking of love affairs, there's someone closer to home who needs a little action." She smirked at me, and I tried to kick her under the table, but since I was wearing flip-flops, it didn't really work. I could feel my face heating up.

"You can't be speaking of yourself," Johnny said to Bella, taking a sip of his Coke. He clearly hadn't noticed her smirk in my direction. "I hear you and Robbie Fishberg swapped spit just last week."

"Yeah," I jumped in, happy to turn the attention back on Bella. "I think there's a *kernel* of truth in that rumor."

"Look." Bella tossed her long layered hair out of her face. "It was over before it even began with Rob Fish*bert*. Three words: braces, comma, popcorn in. How did you even know that — Rob doesn't go to Northside!"

"I am ubiquitous," Johnny answered, patting his mini video camera. "I know all."

"Well, that's just creepy. Anyway, I was talking about *Lisi*. Can't you see she is just radiating *desire*?"

I slurped my Coke and studied the table, my cheeks burning. Johnny took off his glasses, which I always say make him look a little geeky. He wiped them off on his shirt and pretended to study me for a second. Johnny always looks at things very intensely. He has these very powerful dark eyes — I think it has to do with his making films.

"What?" I finally asked.

"Nah," he said, laughing. "I don't detect any of these so-called desire radiations — must be a trick of the light."

Thankfully, the pizza arrived then. "Anyway, Lisi's far too good for any of the male selection around here, methinks." Johnny ruffled the top of my head before reaching for a slice.

Was he making fun of me now? I tried to smooth my hair back.

"Fine." Bella pouted. "No one ever takes me seriously. I'm cool with that. Anyway, Johnny, if you are so ubi — whatever, then do *you* know what's going on between our homecoming king and queen?" Her eyes darted over our shoulders and we both turned to look at the same time.

Brett and Mason's table. Clearly, Bella had been scoping out Mason, since he was her new BT, for reasons I still had yet to uncover. But of course my eyes went immediately to Brett, who was sitting next to Mason, running his hand through his gorgeous light brown hair. Even slumped in his seat, he looked manly and yet . . . tortured. He seemed sort of stormy and upset, like he'd just heard really bad news. My heart started pounding.

Looking at Brett was like looking at the sun — it was hard to see anything else for a couple seconds afterward. But when my head cleared, I noticed something unusual. I quickly swiveled back around to face Bella.

"He's not sitting with Jacqueline!" I whispered. My heart was pounding *inside* my ears, like I couldn't hear myself think.

Jacqueline and Brett were *always* at the same Vinnie's table. Always! Usually tasting more of each other's faces than of any actual pizza . . . but today Jacqueline was sitting with the rest of the Fly Girls, Northside's dance team (glorified cheerleaders), at a table near the main cash register. She and the girls were huddled together, gossiping. They kept sending evil glances over at Brett's table, so *something* was definitely up.

"Do you think something is going on between them? Or rather, *not* going on?" Bella raised her perfectly shaped eyebrows suggestively.

"Shhh!" I said. I was just as intrigued. No, scratch that, I was *way more* intrigued — more than Bella could know. *Did they break up?* "He's going to know we're talking about him," I added. I was too agitated to even look at the pizza, which Johnny was devouring.

"Please chill," Bella said, between bites of her slice. "They're, like, five tables away."

"Who is?" asked a familiar voice.

We all looked up to see a hipster girl standing next to our table. We stared for a few seconds.

Then it clicked.

"Mo!" Johnny was the first to exclaim. "Rad new look!"

Gone were Mo's normally very controlled pale ringlets. She'd let her hair go wild and now it was in this trendy 'fro style that I never would have thought would work. She had also traded in her normal uniform of baggy jeans and T-shirts with funny sayings, and now wore an itty-bitty vest over a white tank top and skinny jeans. She looked like Kate Hudson, but more emo. It was kind of surreal.

"Holy hotness, what happened to you in Paris, girl?" Bella gasped, scooting over to make room.

Mo smiled cautiously and shrugged. "You like? PS?" *PS* meant "pinky swear."

"We love," I jumped in, hooking my pinky finger into hers. "You look *tres* Next Top Model. The vest is so cute!" And it was true. Mo did look great. I was impressed. Very impressed.

Also very shocked. Mo had never seemed to really care about her looks before, and I had zero idea what would have inspired the change. Wouldn't she have at least e-mailed from France if she'd had a sudden inspiration to get a complete makeover, rather than just showing up her first day back from break looking like a total stranger?

Still, it was great to have her back. Despite all the other changes, she still wore no makeup and had that smile in her eyes like she was sharing a silly joke with you and no one else.

"What brought on this metamorphosis?" Bella asked, and I couldn't help wondering if she was as weirded out by it as I was — if there were a chance she, too, felt a sudden pang of . . . jealousy?

Not exactly how I was used to feeling around Mo.

But Mo just shrugged in her slightly awkward Mo way. "Oh, I dunno, I guess I had inspiration in Paris! Besides, it's just that I decided to wear clothes that fit me for once. Except I'm beginning to think these pants are constricting my breathing!" She blushed a little. "Okay, so I succumbed to the wiles of H&M. Enough about that. Can't we talk about something exciting like Spring Carnival?" Mo asked, bouncing a little on her side of the booth as she ripped a piece of bacon off a slice of pizza, folded it, and shoved it in her mouth. "Mmmm," she said, chewing with her mouth slightly open.

I was strangely comforted to see that, despite her new look, Mo still ate the same way — like no one was watching. It was always kind of gross but kind of fascinating.

"EXACTLY," Bella said, clearly relieved to have the conversation back on something that involved her. "I've already heard so many *delicious* ideas drifting around. It's going to be so hard to compete this year!"

Every year, Northside High School hosts Spring Carnival. It's usually held about three weeks after spring break, right before everybody starts going into final exam study mode. We pretty much go all out for the carnival because it's a fund-raiser for the school but half the earnings go to charity. The faculty plans the event, and they bring in rides and snack stands and get as many student clubs and organizations as possible to open different booths. There's always a band — usually a local group — plus a Ferris wheel, and when it gets dark, there are fireworks, and they show a movie on this huge screen they hang down from the football field's goalposts.

Last year the school apparently earned forty-seven thousand dollars. I'm not really sure how, except that parents were encouraged to contribute funds, too. Usually, as extra incentive, they try to offer some kind of prize for the booth that earns the most money.

"I heard the Asian Society is having a karaoke booth again," I said, starting to get a little excited as I grabbed a slice of pizza.

"Oh, I know!" said Mo, bouncing more. "Let's just hope the machine doesn't malfunction again!"

It wasn't technically a malfunction — two years ago some seniors pulled a prank and programmed the karaoke machine to only play dirty lyrics. It was hilarious for about four minutes, until the assistant principal came and shut it down.

"I saw on Facebook that someone's bringing in a palm reader?" I added, definitely getting into the discussion. I love traditions, for one thing. And last year, Spring Carnival was amazing because Mo and Bella and I decided to help out with the French Club's booth. Mo was the only one in the French Club, but they allowed me and Bella to join them. We were just selling crepes but it was super fun to throw around the dough and to talk to all these people one never otherwise would. Or at least, *I* never otherwise would. Bella talks to pretty much everyone at our school. Johnny has his pockets of people to socialize with. Mostly way geekier guys. But me? I'm the kind of person who pretty much only talks to people if they talk to me first.

"Okay, okay, focus," Bella said and waved her hands around. "I have a proposition, which is that we host our *own* booth this year."

"Oooh. Can it be an interview booth?" Johnny asked. We all rolled our eyes. Johnny is obsessed with interviewing as many people as possible for his mockumentary, which is going to be some kind of exposé about the "real" high school experience.

Molly played with a button on her new vest. "Guys, I think having our own booth is an amazing idea." She smiled.

"I'm in!" I cheered, holding up my Coke glass. The others held up theirs and we clinked.

As I looked at their smiling faces, I thought, *This might be my chance to actually talk to Brett.* The idea made me giddy and excited. I mean, yeah, he was sitting not twenty feet away from me at this very moment, but he might have been a galaxy away. It was all about *context*. You don't just go up to people, especially if they are one of the Populars, and blurt out, "Hey, how's it going? I think you're extremely attractive and we have a lot in common and I have already planned our wedding. Oh, by the way, I'm Lisi." You have to have the right context for addressing them. At least, I do.

And maybe the right booth at Spring Carnival would be just that.

Chapter 3

Monday, 8 a.m.

As we drove around the flag circle Monday morning, I saw a big painted banner hanging between two trees that read SPRING CARNIVAL 3 WKS AWAY — SIGN UP NOW!

"Oh my God, we HAVE to decide on our booth, guys! You know I can't handle suspense," Bella breathed excitedly as we filed out of Johnny's car. "See you at assembly!" she called, dashing off, no doubt to get a head start on her plans to woo Mason.

I followed Johnny as we hurried toward the main school doors, my thoughts preoccupied by Brett and his mysterious status with Jacqueline. Why had he looked so angst-ridden at Vinnie's? Last night I dreamed that I had wild crazy hair like Mo's new style and I was running through this field and then I saw Brett and he had tears in his eyes. But he looked at me disgustedly for some reason and then I realized I was completely naked, and woke up. I was so caught up in trying to analyze this dream and wondering if I'd see Brett in the halls today that when Johnny stopped abruptly, I practically crashed into him.

"Hey," he said, turning around. I stared at his red Organized Chaos T-shirt. He wore it all the time, usually over a long-sleeve shirt in colder weather.

"Hay is for horses," I answered, and then remembered Bella's pony impression from last night and grinned a little. "What's up?" I asked, looking up at him. We were always the same exact height until Johnny's growth spurt last year. Now he's way taller than me, even if I wear Claire's heels (which I rarely do).

"Are you gonna let me interview you today?" Johnny had been pestering me about this for the last few months now. He was collecting as many personal interviews as he could, and I'd sorta promised him I'd do one after break.

I tugged on my hair. "I told you I'm not ready. I feel weird about it. Why don't you get Bella to do hers?" Sometimes it makes me nervous when Johnny gets up in my face like this. It's something about extended eye contact — it makes me all jittery.

Johnny shrugged and let his hands drop from my shoulders. "You kidding? I've got, like, twenty straight minutes of her yammering already on there." He grinned his signature Johnny grin, wide and slow. "Come on, we're late," he said, grabbing my backpack strap and pulling me toward the school.

"For a very important date," I said, immediately feeling immature for quoting *Alice in Wonderland*.

I heard the bell ring just as Johnny and I parted ways in the hall, the front doors — covered in sparkly Spring Carnival signs — swinging shut behind us.

Between everyone catching up on what everyone else did over spring break and speculating about the plans for this year's carnival, the morning went by in a breeze and suddenly it was one o'clock and assembly time.

I entered our large, airy auditorium, which hasn't ever been renovated from when the school was built in, like, the early 1900s. It's super old and gothic-looking. I glanced around at the faces of all the other students filling the seats and milling about in the aisles. The Stu Co kids all sat in the first rows, then the freshmen gathered around close to the front, actually paying a modicum of attention to what was going on. Everyone else was left to the chaos of fighting for seats either near the back or along the thick-curtained windowsills.

I finally spotted Mo's crazy blond head. She and Johnny had snagged prime seats near the second window from the back, and I made my way through the jostling crowd to sit by them. Mo had her cute pointy shoes — clearly brand-new — propped up on the seat in front of her and was giggling at something Johnny was saying. He was gesturing wildly. Johnny tells really good stories. As I approached, he was just finishing an elaborate imitation of this physics teacher everyone hates, Mr. K. I'm not actually sure what the K stands for — I don't take physics. I like to think I'm slightly less of a geek than Johnny, though I have my geeky tendencies, too.

"Hey, Lisi!" Mo said. "Bubble dubsters?"

Bubble dubsters is this thing Mo and I used to say when we were tiny kids, but it has stuck all these years. I think it came from what she used to call bubble gum — or what I used to call it. Not sure. Anyway, we just say it when we ask the other for gum. I handed her my pack of Dentyne and plunked down on Johnny's other side, and we all looked around for Bella.

Johnny nudged me with his shoulder, and I looked where he was pointing. Bella was standing next to Mason's seat in the back row. Correction: leaning *over* the seat, showing him something in her notebook. Oh jeez. I still hadn't even gotten my head around why she'd decided to go after Mason in the first place.

"Should I go rescue her?" Johnny muttered.

Mo and I laughed. "I don't think she wants to be rescued, unfortunately," I sighed. Bella could be embarrassingly forward when it came to guys. I glanced back again, just as Brett was sliding into the seat on the other side of Mason. Suddenly I got hot all over. And I felt like I had to get Bella out of there. She was too close to

Brett. It's not like I thought she'd try to flirt with him. When she was focused on a BT, it was kind of like tunnel vision. But still, she could potentially do something embarrassing *in front of* Brett.

Luckily, before I could think of how to intercede, our assistant principal, Stanley Grossman, started tapping on the microphone at the podium on the stage. "Ahem, everyone please be seated so we can move forward with assembly."

Bella appeared a moment later, and I moved my pink retro backpack out of the chair I had saved for her. She was not smiling. In fact, she looked incredibly frustrated as she uncapped her cherry Lip Smacker and reapplied. Mo passed Johnny a piece of paper, which he then passed to me. I unfolded it, and it just had a question mark written on it. I showed it to Bella, and she shrugged without looking at the rest of us. I turned toward Johnny and Mo and shrugged, too. Then we all got quiet and focused as The Gross Man, aka Mr. Grossman, began his speech.

"First of all, I hope you all had relaxing vacations" — a few guys at the back of the auditorium inserted some loud hollers when he mentioned the break — "and are ready to plunge into your final quarter terms with renewed energy," he went on, eliciting groans. "From all of the banners and goings-on in the hallways this morning, I know what's on everyone's mind now. The Spring Carnival!"

This time, we all let out a cheer. Even the cynical alterna-types seem to find the carnival exciting.

"I'm going to let Mrs. Weiss tell you more specifically about the rules and regulations of this year's carnival, but first I just want to say that I have faith you'll all be respectful of the school's mission to raise money for charity. This year, we have a high record to live up to, and I want everyone to work together to make this the best event it can be. And now, Mrs. Weiss."

Some kids shouted "Go Wise!" as Mary Weiss (aka Wise) took the podium. We all really like her. She's the head guidance counselor and events coordinator and is probably in, like, her thirties or something. She's got that young librarian act going, where she seems all proper but secretly is totally cool and knows *everything* that goes on in our school. And I mean everything. She knows more gossip than any of us. And so we all have this profound respect for her. And even a slight fear of her, too.

"Hi, students," she said, in her calm voice. "I am pleased to give you some information about this year's carnival. It will be held, as always, on the East and West playing fields adjacent to Warren Street and will be open ONLY to the Northside High community and their guests. The fireworks will take place at nine p.m., to be followed directly by the movie screening held on the West Field. As we all know, Northside High School has a very positive reputation to uphold, which means abiding by school policy is absolutely required of everyone who participates in Spring Carnival. These rules include, but are not limited to, no drinking, no smoking, no vandalism of public property, no theft, no disorderly conduct. . . ." She went on for a while, listing all the major no-no's that could get us into trouble.

Then she finally got to the good stuff, and we perked up again. "This year, as an extra incentive," she said, "we are offering a particularly special prize, generously provided to us by Howard and Frannie Linerfeld." The Linerfelds were one of the richest families in the area and were sponsors of the big theater in Northside, the new private gallery opening in town, and a bunch of other cultural centers.

Everyone got all hushed, and Mrs. Weiss drew out the suspense for as long as possible before saying, "This year's prize, for everyone involved in the booth that earns the most money — and that means everyone who was *pre-registered*, in full attendance, and barring any other punitive circumstances — the prize for the winning booth members is an all-expenses-paid weekend trip to New York City."

Gasps exploded. Bella, Mo, and I all immediately turned to Johnny. It was Johnny's dream to go to Tisch for college, and therefore to visit New York City. Everyone knows New York and LA are the two best places in the world to study film. True to our expectations, Johnny was panting like a happy dog. He whipped his glasses off and literally wiped something off his face — sweat? a tear? — before looking back at all of us seriously and saying, "Girls. We are so doing a Spring Carnival booth."

Bella started squealing and clapping her hands, but Wise was shushing us again. "All group earnings will be calculated according to the number of tickets collected by the booth," she explained. "Any group — whether it's an official student organization or just a group of independent students looking to get involved — must submit their booth proposals no later than this Thursday. After receiving approval from administration, it is up to each group to acquire the necessary supplies, according to their allotted budget. In the case of independent groups, all supplies are considered a personal expense. Any student interested in coordinating more than one booth must have special permission to do so. As usual, we allow one — and ONLY one — guest pass per student. The guest pass must be submitted to the main office at least twenty-four hours prior to the carnival or your guest will not be permitted to enter. Special requests for additional guest passes can be made only through myself or Stanley." Mrs. Weiss glanced at Stanley — er, The Gross Man — and then back out at us. "Other than that . . . have fun, and let's make this the best Spring Carnival NHS has seen yet."

She smiled calmly and left the platform as the rest of us hooted and high-fived.

Yet as my friends and I filtered back out of the auditorium, I was seriously at a loss as to what we were actually going to *do* for our booth. And we only had a couple of days to figure it out.

Chapter 4

Monday, 4p.m.

After school we spent an hour sprawled on a corner of the playing field, analyzing each of our individual skills. Mo is good at science, French, and solving riddles. Bella's strengths are persuasion, flirting, and preparing frozen foods. Johnny's skill is making films and being funny.

And me? I'm a cutter. That sounds darker than it should. I like to chop up pictures and rearrange them. I have a bunch of collages on my walls, inside my closet door, inside the upstairs bathroom, and in boxes under my bed. I make collages for my friends, and they keep them on the inside of their locker doors. I've noticed that sometimes when I'm looking at a cool photo collection or just flipping through a magazine, my right hand starts making a scissor motion. But I'm not like some freaky Edward Scissorhands type. (Although if I can't have my first kiss with Brett, then my second choice would be Johnny Depp.)

Oh, and I guess I'm pretty decent at math, too. But somehow, none of these skills added up, so to speak.

The one thing we did decide on was that there is power in numbers. Especially since we'd be considered an individual group rather than an official student organization, we knew we'd need help. The more people we could get to man the booth with us and support us financially, the better. Unfortunately, Johnny's friends are all in the computer club and would be otherwise occupied at carnival. Bella has hooked up with all her former guy friends and doesn't have many girlfriends besides us. And I have several people I'm friendly with but felt too embarrassed to ask them to help me run a booth that we didn't even know the theme of yet. Finally, Mo agreed to corral some kids from her French class to join our group. Our plan was to assemble them tomorrow and go over the plans for the booth — assuming we came up with an idea by then.

We left it at that, and Bella and I walked home. Johnny and Mo were sticking around to record an interview for his film. I guess he wanted some fresh footage of Mo with her new look.

"I still think my makeover booth is a really good idea," Bella insisted as she climbed up the steps in front of her mom's huge house a little while later.

I stood on the curb and squinted back at her. "Bella, aside from the fact that Johnny would rather eat monkey brains than play with makeup, there's also the fact that you *know* the Art Club will do face painting again, and they have a world-class face painting legacy. How can we compete with that?" It was true, too. A girl who graduated from NHS, like, twenty years ago became the best face painter in the world, according to some article in the *Chicago Tribune*. Random, yes, but it meant the face painting booth was always popular every year. And while Bella was probably the best eyebrow plucker this side of the Mississippi, that wasn't going to sell a huge quantity of tickets.

"Fine." Bella pouted.

"We'll think of something!" I called as I started heading down the block toward my house.

When I got to my driveway, my mom was pulling out in our old Volvo. "Hop in, honey!" she called, rolling down the window.

"Mom, I have homework. Where are you going?"

"Inspiration hunting," she said with a big grin on her face. It was then that I noticed she was still in her paint-covered yoga pants. Yup, she was definitely on the brink of falling into "the zone." Pretty soon she'd be spending so much time in her studio, I probably wouldn't see her for weeks.

"All right," I shrugged. I tossed my bag into the car and hopped in. "Daryl's? Mack's? All Saints?" These were, respectively, the Mom & Pop diner, shoe shiner, and cemetery that my mother liked to frequent for artistic inspiration. Usually if I go with her, we have a little bit of an adventure and then get fast food. That's a good combination. In addition to Slurpees, I also love any food from Wendy's. Weird, I know, but. Yum.

"Let's just drive and see," she said. We both rolled the windows the rest of the way down, even though it was getting to be a nippy evening. There's so much flat land surrounding Northside when you start driving out of the center of town. It's really peaceful. That's one of the reasons I like living in Illinois even if we *are* kind of in the middle of nowhere.

I like driving with my mom. My dad is always explaining complicated things, and he's always got the radio on, and then he'll interrupt himself in the middle of a long speech just to listen to an advertisement. Like I said, he's career-obsessed, so for him, everything relates back to advertising. But with Mom, we can go for ten whole minutes without either of us uttering a word.

It was nearing dinnertime, my stomach was growling, and the wind had gotten too cold so we'd put the windows up by the time we headed back toward town. As we came down the main street, past the little ice cream shops and hardware stores, Mom suddenly pulled up to the side of the road and parked by a trash can.

Set back from the street was this little thrift shop I've seen a dozen times. I used to go in there when I was younger, whenever my antiques-obsessed grandmother came to visit, but I hadn't been in there for I don't know how long.

We entered the tiny, dimly lit shop, and I saw it was packed to the brim with oddball items, like a crazy person's attic. I patted the head of an old-fashioned rocking horse with real yarn hair. When I lifted my hand, it was covered in dust. Ew.

My mom browsed around, wandering the narrow aisle by the register, which could barely be seen because it was hidden by countless strange-looking garden gnomes. I decided to meander over to the back of the store, away from the eerily old woman who seemed to be snoring behind said garden gnomes and register.

I palmed through some beautiful framed photographs in a cardboard box and felt my right hand itching to have a pair of scissors in it. I picked up a pretty little teacup but instantly got paranoid I'd break it, so I put it back down. I finally understood what people meant by the phrase "bull in a china shop." I kept thinking I'd knock something over with my butt.

A dust bunny fell off of an old chandelier and landed on my arm. Slightly grossed out, I shook it off, stepping backward, and as I did so, I bumped into something that rattled loudly. I saw a shadow out of my peripheral vision and turned just as a huge piece of wood — as in taller than me — tottered and fell toward me.

I caught it just in time as my mother called from the front of the shop, "Everything okay back there, Lis?"

"Yeah, Mom, I'm good," I said, pushing the dusty board back against the wall as carefully as possible. I noticed it was painted in stripes and had dark smudges near the top. It also had a big square cut out of the middle like a window. It looked like it had once had words written across it — where the dark smudges were — but I couldn't make out what it had said. I stared at it for a second, wondering why it seemed to remind me of something, and then it hit me — it looked like the façade of a carnival booth! Who knows, maybe it had been used in a past NHS Spring Carnival! The tradition had been going since way before I was born, after all.

Taking this as a sign, I quickly started trying to rub dust off the top part without knocking it over again.

"Honey, ready to go?"

"In just a second, Mom!" I said, wiping faster. I saw a letter. It was an *R*. Then an *I*. Then an *S*. Two *S*'s. Then another *I*. No, wait. That wasn't an *R*, it was a *K*. I stepped back. The sign at the top — ever so faintly — read:

KISSING BOOTH

I don't really believe in omens. But I do believe in inspiration. Mom always says that even in Northside, Illinois, you can find inspiration if you look for it.

*   *   *

"Who's your best friend?" I asked Bella later that night on the phone.

"Um, Ryan Seacrest."

"Turn off the TV and pay attention!"

"Okay," she sighed. "Um, *you* I'm guessing is where you were going with that?"

"And what's your favorite movie?" I went on.

"What is this, twenty questions?"

"Humor me," I said, pacing my upstairs hall.

"Hm. Um, all right. Let's see. Fave flick of all time. *10 Things I Hate About You.*"

"Noooo, your other fave flick," I said, kind of wishing I'd just gotten to the point already. Bella prefers to play along only when she is the one running the game.

"Oh, um. *Clueless*?" Bella loves movies that are spin-offs of old Shakespeare plays or Jane Austen books. It's this random deep-rooted father-abandonment issue, I swear. Her dad was a British literature professor, and he left when she was ten. They never hear from him. She's not really big on classics, and yet for some *strange* reason, she loves every contemporary movie that was once an old British play or novel.

Finally I gave up and wandered back into my bedroom. "How about *She's the Man*?" I prodded. It's a movie that's based on the play *Twelfth Night*.

"Mmmm," Bella murmured. "Channing Tatum is so mind-bogglingly, heart-stoppingly, soul-quenchingly steaming hot. What about it?"

She's right. If I couldn't have my first kiss with Brett Jacobson and I couldn't have my first kiss with Johnny Depp either, then my third choice would be Channing Tatum.

"DUH!" I screamed. "Don't you remember the scene? When Amanda Bynes first meets him and they have their first kiss together and it's the most romantic moment of all time? You know, at the county *fair?*" I realized I was shouting, but I was so excited I couldn't contain myself.

I could tell Bella was processing. I couldn't wait for her words, though. "We're idiots! It was so obvious all along!" I blurted out.

"Oh. My. God. Lisi, are you thinking what I'm thinking?" Bella asked, her voice rising several pitches.

"A kissing booth!" I cried, laughing and hopping up and down. "I got the idea at a thrift store tonight with my mom. I saw an old kissing booth — like a real live honest-to-god kissing booth — it was an antique, I guess, and how in the WORLD did we not come up with this sooner?!"

In my ear, Bella was squealing, "EEE! Kissing boooooth!"

We both laughed and shouted the words *kissing booth* a few more times before we calmed down and Bella sighed a deep sigh of contentment.

We'd seen *She's the Man* a million times, and seriously, the scene where he buys a ticket to kiss her at the kissing booth is one of the sexiest kiss scenes ever caught on film.

"You ARE my best friend in the world. You are my fave-Lisi. I can't wait to tell everyone tomorrow!"

"Me, too!" I said. "I'm gonna IM Mo now."

I hung up with Bella and signed online. Mo is always online.

LJsnippy: have best idea EVER
Mo$MoProb: hey lis im busy
LJsnippy: drumroll pls
Mo$MoProb: i rlly have to go actually
LJsnippy: come on!
Mo$MoProb: dddddddddddddd
LJsnippy: KISSING BOOTH
Mo$MoProb: wha? 4 spring carnival?
LJsnippy: sumthin like that!!! remember "she's the man"?
LJsnippy: hello? you THERE?
Mo$MoProb: cool idea, def. but I should go
LJsnippy: ???
Mo$MoProb: homework . . .
LJsnippy: oh. well howd yr interview w Johnny go?
Mo$MoProb: I really don't . . .
LJsnippy: ?
LJsnippy: . . .
LJsnippy: mo? u ok?

LJsnippy: well, I'll c u at school. good luck w your hw!
LJsnippy: ba!

That was so weird. Mo and Gchat are like conjoined twins. I'd never seen her log out so fast. I mean, she does care a lot more about homework than some people do. Maybe she just had a big assignment. Although it was the first day back from break, so it just seemed a little . . . un-Mo.

Then again, she didn't *look* like her old self anymore either. So who knew?

All I knew was, we were going to have a kissing booth at the Spring Carnival.

And somehow, some way, I was going to get Brett Jacobson to kiss me.

Chapter 5

Tuesday, 3p.m.

"MWAH!" Bella yelled, planting a huge fake kiss on my cheek. "My first deed as Kissing Booth VP is, I'm taking you for a celebration. Come on, it's been ages since we treated ourselves to some Apples & Oranges. As soon as we meet with the rest of the team."

Apples & Oranges is the nail salon in downtown Northside. And the "team" she was referring to was whoever Mo had convinced to help us with our booth. We'd find out when we met up with them outside by the flagpole in fifteen minutes.

Bella linked arms with me as we sauntered down the third-floor hall. The last bell of the day had rung. "I'm going red, definitely red. Maybe a coral red, for spring. No, probably fire engine. Are you thinking Very Cherry?"

Just then, Johnny bounded out of a classroom and caught up to us. "New York Cit-ay, here we come! Way to go, Jared, I had no idea you had it in you," he said, raising an eyebrow at me. I grinned. Even Johnny was on board with the kissing booth idea.

Bella linked her other arm through Johnny's and the three of us headed down the stairs. I felt on top of the world as we threw open the doors from the stairwell to the first floor. The feeling was almost good enough to drown out that tiny voice that had been whispering in my head all morning: *How can you run a kissing booth if you're an NBK?*

"Okay, meet me by the flag?" Bella asked, turning to me.

"Sure," I called as Bella dashed off to her locker. I faced Johnny as other kids rushed by us, jostling to get at their lockers. "After our meeting we're going downtown. Bella wants to do makeover stuff. Wanna come?"

"Hmm," Johnny muttered, pretending to think hard. "Well, much as I *adore* a good pedi-whatever, I have my own plans. Whoa, careful," he said, pulling me out of the way of a large group of freshmen girls who were giggling as they raced toward the main exit.

And then I noticed why they were giggling. Just as I was shoved in the shoulder by a tall person walking by. That tall person being Brett Jacobson. I blushed, hoping Brett hadn't noticed that he'd basically stampeded me. It wasn't like people usually noticed.

"Oh, hey, sorry, Lesley. How's it going?" Brett had stopped and now gave me a huge smile of apology, his pale blue eyes boring into me.

Oh. My. God.

He's talking. To me. He's saying something to me! Brett Jacobson! I shook my head violently, causing my now short hair to swing and hit me in the face, sticking to my gluelike lip gloss. Great. I tried to remove it slyly. While smiling. The result made it seem like I was sort of weirdly scratching at my face.

"Her name is Lisi, not Lesley," Johnny said, clearing his throat. Leave it to Johnny to totally destroy the moment.

"Cool," Brett said. "Mason, I'm gonna mace you in the face if you don't hurry up. You know Pasker is already pissed today."

Oh. Right. We had been standing near Mason Firestone's locker. Brett's best friend. They were late for practice. He hadn't actually stopped to apologize to *me*. Duh.

And yet, I still stood there, speechless, staring as Mason and Brett talked. Brett was a few inches taller than Mason, but Mason was very all-American looking, with his broad shoulders, dark brown hair, and natural golden complexion.

"Hey, Brett," Johnny suddenly said, apparently in an effort to keep the accidental conversation going. "You a Wes fan?"

"What?"

Johnny adjusted his glasses. "Wes Anderson, the director of *The Darjeeling Limited*. You just quoted that 'mace you in the face' line that Jason Schwartzman says."

"Yeah, man, hilarious movie. Mason, *dude*?" Brett said, turning again to Mason's locker, where Mason was squatting near the floor, trying to sort out which books to stuff into his L.L.Bean leather sack along with his baseball mitt.

"Well," Johnny persisted, "if you're into those kinds of movies, maybe you'd want to do an interview for me. I'm making a documentary of our school — ya know, basic questions about the social nuances of NHS." Johnny looked at Brett hopefully. He'd gotten interviews with a few semi-Populars but so far no one as popular as Brett. At least, not as far as I knew.

"Mason, you could come, too," Johnny added. I could tell he was trying to play it cool but was actually excited at the prospect of getting interviews with seniors into his film. Meanwhile, I was standing there like a statue, completely stunned and unable to speak.

"Like an interview? Sure, whatever." Brett shrugged. "After practice."

"Sweet," Johnny said.

Brett shrugged again as Mason stood up with his stuff and then the two of them strutted off toward the gym, leaving us both with our mouths open. Why hadn't I said anything about the kissing booth? Had I missed my chance? Watching him walk away made me want to cry. I stared at Brett's arms as they swung along at his sides, wanting more than anything to run up and take his hand and fall into step, like we had always meant to be walking the halls together.

I figured Johnny was shocked that Brett had said yes to contributing to his film. But that wasn't so surprising, since Brett was clearly used to being a public figure, at least by Northside standards.

No, what was surprising was, *Brett knew who I was.* Sure, he'd been slightly off with my actual name, but he'd been close. He recognized me, at least. That was definitely something. That meant something. Didn't it?

"Hey, bonehead. Or should I say *Lesley.*" Johnny wiggled my right ear.

"Careful, these are my sister's earrings," I said, pulling back from Johnny to reclaim my ear. I realized I'd been gaping in the direction of Brett and Mason. I adjusted the weight of my backpack as though I'd simply been stretching my neck.

"Are you obsessed with him or something?" Johnny asked.

"What? Am I what? Obsessed with who? I mean, why do you ask?" I stuttered.

Did he know?

"Well, you'd be one of many, apparently," Johnny said, lifting an eyebrow. I noticed recently that when he raises his eyebrows, he looks just like Casey Affleck. Sometimes I wonder if he practices it in front of a mirror and knows it looks cool.

"Whatever," I said, giving Johnny a push toward the door. "You're the one who was practically drooling and *begging* him to be in your film. Anyway, don't you have some place to be?"

"I beg for nothing," Johnny said, straightening his inside-out black T-shirt and jabbing me in the arm before sauntering away. "See ya by the flagpole."

I hurried to my locker and saw a sign stuck to its puke-green door. It was a sign made out of bright red construction paper that said GET YOUR SPRING CARNIVAL ON in glitter pen. I grabbed my books and quickly stuffed them all into the pink vinyl backpack I'd begged for at Christmas last year but already hated. Retro was totally out. Oh well. The only thing that mattered in that moment was Brett knew who I was! I slammed the locker door and stared again at the sign.

Brett would buy a ticket. Somehow I'd convince him to. Then he'd stand in a long line, anxiously running his hands through his light brown hair like he was always doing. None of his friends would be around. Then he'd get to the front of the line, and he'd shift his weight and say "What's up?" Then he'd look deeply into my eyes, his own blue-gray eyes shining back at me with longing. Finally he'd say, "I've been waiting for this chance forever. You're, like, the coolest girl I know." Then I'd close my eyes as he slowly leaned in toward me, just like Channing Tatum.

And then . . . what? Would I be a good kisser? Would I know what to do? Or would I mess up and ruin everything?

I wondered if this fantasy could really come true. There'd always been that certain something about Brett, beyond just good looks and a confident personality, that made me feel like I understood him.

The moment I realized how right we were for each other was in the geometry class we had together my freshman year, his sophomore year. He sat right in front of me because we were seated alphabetically: Jacobson. Jared. All that year I'd stare at the back of his neck, overhearing his conversations with his friends in the class, wondering what it would be like to talk to him eye to eye.

And then one day we had a test and he'd swiveled around in his chair to borrow a pencil from me. He winked when I gave him one, and after that, it became a habit that for every quiz and test, I would lend him a pencil and he'd wink at me. I'd always thought that wink meant something. It wasn't just a wink. It was a symbolic gesture. Like, even though we were worlds apart socially, he saw something in me across all those barriers.

I shook my head as I raced through the main school doors and out onto the sun-splashed front quad. The group was already gathered by the flagpole. There were seven of us: me, Bella and Johnny, plus four recruits — Celeste Bachiavalli, the know-it-all with beautiful red hair, from Mo's language lab; Celeste's best friend, Sarah Singer, with the totally grating laugh; some seriously dorky-looking guy named Dan who, from the looks of him, was only there because he was in love with Celeste; and this girl named Petra Wu whom I knew from English. Petra was one of those girls who joined every club she could. Everything was about building her résumé for college, but who cared? We needed people.

With Mo, that would make eight people. Perfect for a kissing booth. That way we could work in shifts and enjoy the rest of the carnival during other people's time slots. But where *was* Mo? I still hadn't figured out why she'd sounded so bizarre online last night, and now she was nowhere to be found.

I looked at Bella. "You seen Mo?" I asked. Bella shook her head. The rest of the "crew" looked like they were getting restless.

"Should we start without her?" Bella asked.

Johnny looked like he was about to say something, then paused. "Yeah, let's just jump right in. I saw Mo earlier today and she . . . wasn't feeling well."

Okaaaaaaay. That was totally suspicious. Mo was never sick without telling me. We had a tradition involving chicken soup and Mad Libs. When I got chicken pox in third grade, Mo spent every single day after school with me until we'd filled three books of Mad

Libs and she'd caught the chicken pox. Then I spent every day with *her*.

The seven of us decided to get down to business. We sat cross-legged on the grass by the flagpole to develop our rules for the booth. Petra was good to have around — due to all of her experience in clubs and such, she knew all about what the administration was willing to approve. She was the one who insisted that we'd have to specify "cheek kisses only."

Bella groaned and Celeste rolled her eyes. I was a bit deflated, too. But I could see Petra's point. The booth couldn't be Make-out Central.

"Why don't we add it to our list of rules, and then just use our own judgment when the time comes," I suggested.

So far, our list of rules read:

One ticket is good for one kiss
No repeat customers
Must be on opposite sides of the booth itself
No hanky-panky — keep hands to self (this rule had
    all of us cracking up)
Cheek kisses only

Satisfied that we'd be able to meet Mrs. Weiss's approval, we dropped off our form in the office and said our good-byes. Johnny slapped me and Bella five, then went off to find Brett and Mason for his interviews.

I had to physically hold Bella back from following him. She was dying to know what Mason would reveal.

"We're getting our nails done now, remember?" I said, steering her back outside.

"You're never any fun," Bella sighed. But she had a smile on her face.

Chapter 6

Tuesday, 4p.m.

"Okay." Bella was brushing her hair as we marched down the sidewalk toward Northside's downtown area. "What's that gel stuff they put on your teeth at the dentist and it comes in, like, mint or strawberry but it all just tastes like chemicals?" she asked.

"Fluoride?" I offered.

"Yeah, that's totally what it felt like! Who knew Jeff was practicing to be a dental hygienist? Or maybe he just has OCD and felt the need to count each of my teeth with his tongue."

"You're so mean, Bells."

"I know. But seriously. I'm not making another hook-up appointment with *Doctor* Jeffrey any time soon. It's too bad, though, because he has killer taste in jeans, a trait that's hard to find in a man. Oh well." Bella heaved a deep, melodramatic sigh.

I took off the black cashmere cardigan that I had borrowed from Claire's closet, and tied it around the strap of my backpack. The afternoon sun felt warm and comfortable on my shoulders. I hoped it was helping to preserve my tan.

I adjusted the strap of my tank top. "So, um, why were you kissing Jeff in the first place? Sorry if I missed something."

Bella shrugged. "Well, I saw Brett and Mason walking to the field while I was waiting for you all by the flag, and Jeff was just there. There weren't that many other people around. I figured, if I'm going to have a moment where I can get Mason's attention, I might as well make the most of it, right?"

"So you just grabbed Jeff and started kissing him? In broad daylight? Who does that?" I asked, squinting. It was hard to believe Bella and I were best friends sometimes.

"I do! I wanted to make Mason jealous, and you know how Jeff kind of had a thing for me in third grade," Bella answered, matter-of-factly, as if this were (a) common knowledge and (b) an acceptable excuse. "So I just told him he had something on his shoulder, then I leaned in and, well, you know?"

I nodded. But I didn't know. That was the whole problem.

Bella put her hairbrush back into the front pocket of her backpack as we arrived at Apples & Oranges. The door jingled as it closed behind us, and two women stood up from behind the nail counter.

"Hello, come in, come in," the shorter of the two women encouraged, waving us over.

"Mani/pedi," Bella said matter-of-factly.

"Yes, yes, pick a color," the woman told us. She pointed to the wall of polishes ranging from Sugar Daddy to Goth Chic.

The shop had the familiar smell of fruity soap, flowers, and the tang of nail polish remover. It wasn't hot enough out yet for air-conditioning, but a ceiling fan whirred over our heads, keeping the air light and crisp. I chose Sugar Plum for my toes, and the woman guided us over to two automatic massage chairs with tubs at the bottom. She began running the warm water to fill the tubs.

I kicked off my shoes and let my feet slide into the bubbling water as I leaned back into the leather chair.

"Here," Bella said, leaning over my armrest and hitting a little button on a remote. The chair began to rumble and knead, jostling my head so it seemed like I was nodding yes.

"Is there a way to slow it down?" I asked, fiddling with the other buttons.

"So, Lisi," Bella said, relaxing into her own chair, "you trust me, right?"

"What do you mean, Bells? Of course. I mean, shoot, this chair is freaking out. Oh, wait, okay, that's better," I said, finding the GENTLE ROLL setting. "Trust you to what?"

"I don't know, I'm just asking." Bella looked at her hands and sighed. It wasn't like her to be thinking something and not just say it out loud.

I tried to look Bella in the eyes but my chair was moving my head too much. I gave up and leaned back again, letting my eyes close. "I can't believe we're already in the final quarter of junior year," I muttered. "Isn't it weird how fast high school goes by?"

After this year, Brett would be gone — graduated. What would I do then? I couldn't picture what it'd be like walking down the halls knowing he wasn't at school with us anymore, nothing to make me nervous and excited, nothing to speculate about. No more newspaper articles with his name printed at the bottom for me to read and reread, dissecting for any clue into what he was really like. I was dying for the next issue of the paper to release on Thursday. Maybe there'd be some hint as to what was going on between Brett and Jacqueline.

"So?" Bella had apparently asked me something.

"Hmm?" I responded, shivering a little as the woman scrubbed the bottom of each of my feet with a rough sponge. I hadn't had a pedicure since the past summer. I'd forgotten how relaxing it was.

"I was *saying*, who do you want to kiss?"

"What do you mean?" Suddenly I felt a knot of dread creep into my stomach. I hoped the nail ladies weren't listening.

"If you could pick one boy at our school to be your first kiss, who would it be?" Bella asked. Why did she have to just *announce* the fact that I had never kissed anyone? In public! Like my NBK status was just common knowledge, when in actuality it was *totally mortifying*.

"I dunno." I shrugged. "I've told you, I really haven't thought about it. I figure it'll just happen if it happens, right?" I couldn't look at her when I was lying.

"Why don't I believe you?"

"I don't know, Bella, why don't you believe me?"

"Because despite all odds, you came up with the kissing booth. This is something I've been mulling over all day. I mean, I *know* how you get. I'm your best friend after all."

I didn't say anything.

"Not like anyone will be able to *tell* you've never been kissed. It's not *that* obvious to be a first-timer. But that's not the point. The point is, normal Lisi would be all scaredy-cat about kissing booth, not Miss Number One Champion. So I've been thinking about it and there must be a reason. And then I realized that reason must be — DUH — a boy. So," Bella said smugly as she handed her Fishnet Red bottle to the pedicurist, "spill."

I glanced at the glass door we'd come in through. I could run for it. But I'd have to run in these plastic green Apples & Oranges flip-flops, and they hadn't even finished my top coat. Very clever of Bella to trap me first, *then* interrogate. She'd always been a tad more clever than I'd given her credit for.

I knew I *should* just tell her. That would be what a best friend would do. But every time I thought about saying the words *I like Brett* out loud, I felt my throat close up. I *knew* that Bella would make a big deal out of it. She'd tell everyone. And then everyone in our school would eventually know how desperate and pathetic I was.

And then *no* boy would kiss me, *ever*.

I couldn't risk the humiliation. Not when I was this close to finding a way to get Brett to kiss me at the kissing booth without anyone ever having to find out that it had been my master plan all along.

I turned to Bella. "There's nothing to spill. And anyway, most of the boys in our school are lame." Well, at least it wasn't a complete lie. I rolled my eyes.

Bella blew her extra-long bangs out of her face.

"Come on," I continued, "let's discuss something more interesting. Did Mason react when he saw you kissing Jeff today?"

The Apples & Oranges women helped us out of our massage chairs so we could plod over to the nail counter and get our fingernails done. We were careful not to bump our freshly painted toes on anything.

Bella stared straight at the wall as she held out her hands to be cleaned and rubbed with lotion. She didn't say anything to me.

"Well?"

Bella shrugged but still didn't look over at me.

"Oh, come on, Bella, don't be like that. Tell me about Mason."

I could see Bella's shoulders loosen and knew she was going to give up her fight. Thank goodness, because I couldn't have her *and* Mo acting weird at the same time.

"Fine," she sighed. "Mason is . . . Mason is, I don't know, *impossible*."

"Bells, for you anything's possible," I said, laughing a little.

"I don't know, Lisi, he's proving more difficult than the others. He didn't even sneak the TINIEST peek when Jeff and I were, you know. He just kept walking! Believe me, I was scoping him out over Jeff's shoulder. I just can't believe he acts like he doesn't *notice* me! I mean, today in homeroom I asked if I could copy his notes for chem and he was all 'they're in my locker.'"

"Well, maybe they were really in his locker," I suggested.

"Yeah, SO not the point, Lis. He's not picking up on my *vibe*!"

"He's probably playing hard to get, then."

"Boys don't play hard to get. They play sports, they don't play head games. That's girl territory only. Come on, haven't I taught you anything?" After our hands were properly softened up, Bella handed her nail person the credit card her mom let her use. "It's on me, Lis. It was my idea."

"You rock my world," I said, watching as my manicurist applied the first base coat. "And," I said, feeling generous — it was amazing how Bella could do that to me. One minute I wanted to flee her like the plague, and the next to give her a huge hug — "I am sure you will rock Mason's world, too, once he wakes up and smells the fabulousness."

"You think?" Bella asked.

"Bella, it sounds like you really *like* him!" I tried to think about what made Mason different from the other guys Bella had been interested in, but there wasn't much that was special about him. Maybe that was the reason she liked him. He was so . . . *normal.* "I've never seen you so stressed about a guy before. And we both know there've been plenty of opportunities for it."

"It's just that I've never had this problem before. My tactics *always* work. Maybe I'm losing my edge. Clearly I need to start stepping up my game."

"Maybe you should just tell him you like him or something," I said, feeling suddenly wise. "You know, go for the whole honesty approach. I hear it's all honorable and stuff."

Bella *hmmphed.* "No, you have to help me seduce him. That's the only answer."

"Are you sure?"

"Positive."

I gazed out past the mobile of fake apples and oranges dangling by the windows. The sky was already darkening. I wanted to tell Bella that just confronting

Mason — telling him her true feelings — was probably the best way to figure out what he was thinking. I knew Bella was gutsy enough to approach anyone. But I kept my mouth shut.

After all, I was the last person who should be preaching about honesty.

Chapter 7

Tuesday, 7 p.m.

I rolled over on Claire's old four-poster bed and switched my phone to my other ear. "But what exactly *is* sociology? I mean, is it the same thing as, like, *psy*chology?"

Claire had the fluffiest pillows of anyone. They were made out of real feathers, but the fabric was starting to fall apart, so they were kind of prickly to lie on. I tugged at the end of a feather that was poking through.

"Soc," Claire said from the other end of the line — but she said it like "soash," which must be the college way to say it — "is the study of how people behave, kind of."

"Like how they act?" I pulled the feather out and twirled it.

"Well, it's more specific than that of course, Lis. It's more like, what people watch on TV or the patterns of how they respond to it in a social context, or —"

"SO unfair! You get to study what people watch on TV?"

"I just meant for example. Obviously it's way more serious and complicated than that. But, it *is* pretty cool. I just turned in a paper on *The Simpsons*. But it was like, about the escapism of animation as a mode of questioning social mores."

"Oh." I blew the feather out of my hand, and it swirled down to Claire's soft green rug. Her whole room was decorated in sage and white. Sage-green curtains, white desk, sage pillow covers, white bedspread, everything matchy-matchy. "So is that going to be your major or something?" I asked, picking up one of Claire's old stuffed animals — a koala named Koko — and looking into its tiny marble eyes.

"Not sure yet. Anyway, what's going on with you?" Claire asked. I could hear a clanging sound in the distance, behind Claire's voice.

"Not much, as usual. Well, actually Bella and Mo and I are doing this thing for Spring Carnival and it's pretty crazy but I don't know, it could either be extremely amazing or utterly humiliating and I can't quite figure out which."

"Humiliating like how?" Claire asked, clanging more. It sounded like a billion pots and pans.

"Um, like, well . . . Like with boys or whatever." Koko stared back at me blankly.

"Does Bella want you to ask someone out at Spring Carnival?"

"Well, no. It just sort of has to do with this booth we're doing, which kind of involves, like, I mean, *kissing*."

"A kissing booth?" Claire laughed. "That's so adorable! I'm surprised the admin is letting you guys do something so *racy*, though."

"Well, it's going to have a lot of rules, so it's not that racy or anything. It's just that it's, I don't know, embarrassing, right? Or do you think it's cool?"

"Why would it be embarrassing?"

I put Koko back on the bed and wandered over to Claire's dresser, opening her old jewelry box. "It's just" — I paused, trying to take Claire's earrings out of my ears with the hand that wasn't holding my cell — "who would want to kiss me anyway?"

"Lisi!" Claire said, jangling more pots.

"What?"

"Plenty of people want to kiss you. Why wouldn't they? You're hot. Plus you're a great person. Double whammy, right?"

"Claire, are you salsa dancing with a set of pots and pans or what?" I interrupted.

"No, Mitch and I are making Bolognese sauce for dinner."

"Don't you live in a dorm? And what's Bolognese?"

"They have a kitchen on every floor. You know what Bolognese is."

"No, I don't," I said, sitting down at Claire's desk.

"It's like red sauce with meat in it."

"Well, why didn't you just say that?" I opened and closed some of Claire's drawers. Old papers. Pens without ink. Nothing interesting.

"Because it's called Bol — whatever. What is your problem? Why are you freaking out about boys? Why don't you just ask out that Brett kid. Aren't you still in love with him?"

"Claire! God, can you not say that so loudly?"

"It's just Mitch and me here. Right, Mitch?" Claire's tone of voice changed ever so slightly, kind of like it did when she was addressing our neighbor Miss Hadley's pug.

I could hear muffled movement and then Mitch in the background saying, "Go get him, Lisi!"

"He has a girlfriend!" I protested, blushing. "Well, at least, he *did*. And I'm not his type. I mean, what if I'm not? How do I get him interested?"

"How could you *not* be someone's type?"

"Claire, you sound like Mom."

"I'm just saying, what makes you so *sure* he wouldn't like you?"

"I just don't know, okay? I'm not on his radar." I thought about Brett's apologetic grin when he bumped into me in the hall earlier that day. I wondered if he and Jacqueline had really broken up. They hadn't been seen together in the halls at all on Monday or Tuesday. "I'm just worried he doesn't see me as dating material. Nobody at Northside does."

"Hon, it sounds to me like you don't see *yourself* as

dating material. I mean, why not? What's so freaking bad about you? Well, besides that you steal all of my stuff when I'm not home," Claire added drily.

I put down the handbag I'd been considering taking off of Claire's closet door. "It's not that there's anything bad about me, per se," I answered. "It's just . . . I'm just. . . . I don't know . . ."

"Mitch, stop!" Claire started giggling like crazy. "Oh my God, he's getting sauce *everywhere*. I really gotta go."

". . . I'm *boring*," I muttered quietly.

"Say hi to mom and dad, and I'll call on the weekend, 'kay? Mitch, you're so crazy!" Claire laughed, clicking off the phone.

I walked out of Claire's bedroom. It was cold in there anyway. I wandered down the upstairs hall, dragging my slippers along the dark wood floorboards. Then I turned around, went back to Claire's room, grabbed Koko under my arm, marched into my own room, and set Koko next to my pillow.

"MOM," I called, coming down the stairs. "What's for dinner? Is Dad home?"

My mom opened the door to her studio with one hand and then went back to her canvas. "I just ordered, babe. From the new Thai place."

"I wanted pasta," I said, leaning into the doorway of the studio.

"I thought you love Thai? And dad's eating at the office."

"Did you get spring rolls?"

"Of course. Here, we'll at least use real dishes," Mom said, rinsing off her paint-covered hands in her studio sink and then leading me into the kitchen. Her light brown hair was tucked up into a messy ponytail, and she was wearing her silk pajamas but with a paint-flecked flannel shirt over them. I cleared a pile of Dad's client giveaways from the middle of the kitchen table and Mom handed me two bowls to set out, forks and glasses. I put the red kettle on for tea. When the door-bell rang, my mother gave me a twenty to pay the delivery boy and then we both sat down to eat.

"Ooh, this is spicier than the old Thai place," Mom commented, mixing more rice into her red curry.

I bit into a spring roll, and bits of its crispy shell fell all over the table. I picked up some of the crumbs and thought about Bella, how she picked up boy after boy like they were so many crumbs on a table. Why was it so much harder for me? What was I so afraid of anyway?

"Lisi, honey, what are you doing in about two weeks?"

"Um . . ." *Two weeks?* The Spring Carnival was in two weeks — well, two and a half. Did Mom somehow know about the kissing booth?

"'Cause I have a surprise!" she said, beaming. *Hmm*, well, the surprise couldn't possibly be that the school had called to tell her that her daughter was the main instigator behind the kissing booth and thereby jeopardizing the Spring Carnival's moral agenda or something. She wouldn't be smiling quite so big if that were the case.

"I'll give you a hint. Howard Linerfeld." She had a strange gleam in her eye.

"Who?"

"You know, the new gallery in town? The one with the 'Grand Opening' banner that's been up there for ages? Well, sweetie, guess who's been given a show on May third? They want my *Shells* series!"

"Mom, that's so awesome!" I smiled, reaching over to hug her. There were framed awards all over our house with Cecilia Newton (Mom's maiden name) printed on them. I know she is really talented. When I was younger, I used to think Mom's paintings were kind of, well, weird. Because they looked almost realistic, but then there was always something you couldn't put your finger on that made it not the real world at all. *Now*, of course, I was old enough to realize it was exactly that thing you couldn't put your finger on that made the paintings so special.

"Yeah, this is a big deal, babe," my mother said, washing her curry down with green tea in a Have It Your Way mug. "You'll come, right? And the Deans will come, of course." My mother had gone to art school with Cora Dean — Molly's mom — and now Cora was a successful interior designer. I thought about the fact that I hadn't really spoken to Mo since yesterday afternoon. I had tried calling Mo before I called Claire, but she hadn't answered.

"I need you to help me choose the pieces," Mom went on. "They only have room for four."

"Definitely the one with the green lady," I answered without even having to think. "And maybe that sunset one, because I can tell it's important to you." The *Shells* series was all about these seashells with figures in different colors emerging out of them, which sounds kind of freaky but actually they were really pretty.

"You're right about the sunset one. Thanks, hon. This show has to be perfect." She started clearing the dishes, so I got up to help. I ran the hot water in the sink and squirted soap onto the sponge.

"Mom, it's not like this is your first show or anything. I mean I know it's a nice gallery, but why is this one so important? Are they giving you tons of money for it or something?"

"Well, I haven't done a show in almost four years. I know it seems easy, but there aren't as many independent galleries in the area as there used to be. And the Linerfeld is . . . very prestigious. To tell you the truth," she said, drying off and stacking the plates in the cabinet — now that Claire was away at school, we hardly ever ran the dishwasher — "I'm terrified." She closed the cabinet and pushed some loose strands of hair out of her face.

"Oh." It felt weird that anything would terrify Mom.

Especially something she was obviously good at. "So you didn't actually want it?"

"I want it more than anything. That's precisely why it's terrifying. Don't you think being scared means you really care? That you should commit to it, no matter what?" She leaned back against the counter. She looked tired.

"Yeah, sure. I mean, I guess so." I thought about the kissing booth. Was I scared to do it? Maybe. Well, definitely. But only because it meant I might be able to kiss Brett. And this was both the best thing I could imagine happening and the most frightening. And I was starting to have serious doubts.

After all, I only had a little over two weeks to get Brett to buy a ticket to our booth. And what if he didn't? Or what if he did but it all ended in disaster? What if he didn't end up kissing me, he kissed someone else, or worse, he did kiss me but thought I was a disgusting kisser? What if he did the fluoride thing like Jeff?

"Oh no," my mother gasped, startling me from my thoughts as I handed her a plate. "Honey, your nails! Here, let me see if I can fix it." She dashed into the downstairs bathroom, and I looked down at my hands. The nails on my right hand had smudged from washing the dishes. Mom returned with a bottle of paint remover from her studio — the real thing — and a bottle of light pink, almost sheer polish.

She dragged me over to the kitchen table. "It's not right for French manicures, but better than nothing."

Then the award-winning Cecilia Newton sat down and ever so delicately redid my nails. It was strange seeing my mom paint with such a tiny brush, when she was used to big wild strokes on a canvas.

She lifted my hands and blew lightly to dry the nails.

"There," she said. "All better."

Little did she know, the trouble had only just begun.

Chapter 8

Wednesday, 8a.m.

I grabbed my toast, kissed my mom and dad good-bye, and darted out the front door at the sound of the car honking three times. It was Wednesday morning.

"Where's Thelma, Louise?" Johnny tapped his fingers on the steering wheel as I hopped into the front seat next to him. Usually he drove both me and Bella to school.

"Not riding with us for the time being. It's part of this master plan we were talking about yesterday," I said, buckling in.

It felt good to be in the front seat. The sun came in through Johnny's dirty old windshield and filled the car. It was finally warm enough to be out in the morning without a sweater. I wore my plain black ribbed tank, dark boot-cut jeans, and flip-flops. I noticed Johnny was wearing his black Organized Chaos T-shirt with no other layer underneath. I noticed this because it was strange seeing his pale, muscular arms after a long winter of hibernation. He had freckles on them, even though he didn't have any on his face.

I kicked my feet up onto the dashboard and leaned back.

"Comfy?" Johnny flicked a piece of mud off of my flip-flop. "Hey, nice toes," he said, noticing the Sugar Plum pedi.

"Thanks."

He steered the car out of the driveway and down the road. "So listen," he said, "I really need you to do that interview for me. I'm trying to get to the editing stage, but I need as much material as I can get."

"Johnny, I know, but I seriously have nothing interesting to add." I rolled my eyes and looked out the window. This conversation was getting old.

"Dude, you keep saying that, and I keep telling you I disagree. But anyway, here's the thing. Tisch is having an open house."

"Cool!" I knew how much going to college there meant to him.

"No, not just cool. Like, totally necessary that I be there, with some finished material. But here's the thing, and I know it's going to sound all rah-rah and everything, but I really want us to win that trip to New York. Even if it means making this silly kissing booth idea work."

"Yeah." I nodded slowly. "Me, too. I mean, I want the kissing booth to win." All I could think was that if we got as many people as possible to buy tickets, maybe Brett would be one of them.

"Awesome. So we're on the same page." Johnny glanced over at me with a grin that looked half embarrassed, half wicked. "Well, I know I'll get an interview out of you one of these days. I've got thirty-seven interviews now, including the ones I got yesterday after school from Brett Jacobson and Mason Firestone," he said, keeping his focus on the road. "Speaking of Mason, what's this master plan of Bella's?"

"I call it Plan: Mason Seduction, or PMS."

Johnny raised an eyebrow. "Do I even want to know?"

I grinned. "She wanted to get to homeroom early to set up. I think the plan basically involves making him jealous at all costs. So she's dragging some helpless third person into the equation. I think maybe that guy Jeff Zeigler."

"The guy with the weirdly tight jeans?"

"Apparently she likes his jeans." I laughed. "But that's not the point. She just needs to use someone to get Mason to notice her."

"A classic plot." Johnny shook his head.

"Do you think jealousy actually works, though? I mean, from a guy's point of view?" I asked, as Johnny turned the car around in the front lot. There were no spots, so we headed over toward the back lot, which took a long time because we had to wait for the stoners and skaters to get out of the way.

Johnny was silent as he parked the car. It looked like he was actually thinking hard about the jealousy question — his eyebrows got all wrinkly. Finally he sighed and replied slowly, clearly, choosing his words carefully, "Making someone jealous on purpose, whether it's to attract or hurt them, is manipulative and basically it sucks. I mean, no offense to Bella or anything. It's just . . ."

Whoa. I was really surprised that Johnny had such a strong opinion on the matter. He seemed almost mad! He unbuckled his seat belt, grabbed his backpack and his camera, and turned to me.

"It's just asking for trouble."

Chapter 9

Thursday, 12 p.m.

I sank down to the floor with my back against my locker, clutching the *Northside Outlook*. It was true. Brett was an editor on the paper; he wouldn't have let "Page Seven" print it if it weren't true. It was in the gossip column, right below "KT's unnatural enhancements responsible for food fight" (referring to the little spat that broke out in the caf the day before over Katrina Terrence's new fake boobs, involving her pouring chocolate milk on Brian DeLancy's head). The item I couldn't stop reading said: *BNJ and JSW fairy-tale romance shattered. Now we can all go back to real life.*

Brett and Jacqueline really *had* broken up. It was official!

My hands were getting clammy, so I folded up the paper and stuffed it into my backpack. When I turned around, Bella was standing next to me with her hands on her hips.

"There you are! I'm starving, come on." She pulled me up off the dirty faux marble floor, and we walked toward the cafeteria.

"Have you seen Mo?" I asked as we entered the caf's double doors. A big banner for the Fly Girls' Dance Dance Revolution competition swayed above the entrance.

"Case of the disappearing friend," Bella answered, rolling her eyes at the banner as we passed beneath it. "I have no idea what's gotten into that curly head of hers. To be brutally honest, I'm kinda over it." Bella flipped her long hair over her shoulder as she headed for our usual table.

"Well, maybe she's depressed or something. . . ." I began, then stopped — well, crashed into Bella, really, who had halted suddenly in the middle of one of the aisles between tables. I looked where Bella's gaze was fixed.

It was Mo.

She was twirling a short blond ringlet and whispering with . . . Jacqueline Winslow. At the Fly Girls' table.

Bella muttered something under her breath. I could barely hear but it sounded like, "No eye contact." I was too stunned to have much of a reaction other than finally remembering to close my gaping jaw. Too many confused emotions were racing through my mind.

Mo? Friends with *Jacqueline?* Oh. God. What if Mo told her about my secret crush? She couldn't. Could she?!

Bella turned on her heel and linked arms with me, pulling me quickly in the opposite direction. I glanced back to see Jacqueline laughing in slow motion surrounded by the dance team — and our former best friend. Or at least, those girls always seemed like they were laughing together in slow motion, like their lives were a movie or something. I was too stunned to really think about what this meant. I simply made a mental note to ask Johnny about the proper term for the slow-motion thing.

What was going on with Mo? My stomach tightened. And I couldn't believe Jacqueline could look so happy after breaking up with Brett.

Bella led me straight to the table where Mason, Brett, Jack Kreber, and Dave Hallston sat, downing their hoagies. I felt the color immediately creep into my cheeks, like it did whenever I accidentally came too close to Brett. Just then Brett ran his fingers through his floppy hair and looked up. For a minute it seemed like he actually recognized me — maybe from crashing into me the other day! Oh, the joy of crowded hallways!

I was suddenly excruciatingly aware of breathing really shallow breaths.

"Hey, guys," Bella said. "We just wanted to remind you *in person* about our Spring Carnival kissing booth.

I'd give you a teaser but that just wouldn't be fair to the others," she breathed, leaning slightly over the edge of their table.

I snapped my eyes away from Brett, whose mouth was fixed in the slightest of bemused grins. *He and Jacqueline are broken up.* It was too much. I knew Bella was putting all her energy into this painfully obvious attempt at flirting with Mason, and I knew I had agreed to help Bella get him to notice her, but I just couldn't be an accomplice if it meant totally mortifying both of us in front of Brett. At this very moment, it was possible that she was in fact *ruining* my chance of getting Brett to buy a ticket to our booth.

I thought quickly. *"Leave them wanting more,"* I murmured to my friend in what I hoped was a really subtle fashion. Then I pulled Bella, who seemed to have understood my point, away from the table and out of the cafeteria as quickly as possible.

As soon as we were out in the hallway, however, Bella turned to me. "What's your problem?" she demanded.

"Nothing, I was just, you know . . . we never talk to that table. I thought, better to start out small, work your way up. Or something. Er, play hard to get. Isn't that the plan?"

"Lisi, look, if Mo can shimmy her way into Jacqueline's circle in a mere few days, then we can just as easily get noticed by Mason and all those other guys."

"I thought the whole plan with Mason was to

make him jealous," I pointed out. "Oh, and Johnny said he had an interview for his film with Mason and Brett." I knew I was blushing just saying Brett's name out loud, but I pushed on quickly. "Maybe he'll let us watch it, and you can work more on the strategy."

"Oh, yeah! Did Johnny get him to spill personal stuff? And I guess you're right. I have to play my cards carefully with Mason. He isn't like the others."

"You're right, I'm not like the others," said Johnny, showing up at my side from around the corner. "I can't help it." He shrugged, grinning. "I'm an individual."

Bella rolled her eyes.

"Ladies, why are we headed *away* from the caf? Are we on a no-lunch diet today?"

"Actually," I chimed in, "can we eat in your car today, Johnny?"

Johnny looked at us, clearly pondering whether or not he should inquire further. Then he shrugged again and said, "Delighted. Let me just swing by the vending machines on our way out."

After procuring two bags of sour cream & onion chips, one granola bar, and two packets of Famous Amos chocolate chip cookies, we made our way to the back lot.

Johnny drove in slow, lazy circles around the school as we ate.

"*Please*, Johnny. You *have* to let us see the Mason interview. Why are you being so cryptic?" Bella batted her eyelashes at Johnny and clutched his sleeve.

From the backseat, I avoided looking at the rear-view mirror, where I figured Johnny was probably sending me a glare that meant I shouldn't have reminded Bella about that particular interview. But the thing was, I kind of wanted to watch the interview, too. Okay, I was *dying* to watch it. It might show me something secret about Brett.

"Bella, I'm serious. I can't let anyone see the raw material. It would compromise the artistic integrity. Not to mention violate their confidentiality." Johnny turned the steering wheel under his left palm as he rounded the south corner of the block. With his right hand he held out a Famous Amos bag.

Bella pouted but took one of the cookies anyway.

"Guys, let's talk about how we're going to make the kissing booth win," I said, feeling obligated to change the subject.

"I have to say," Bella said, swallowing her cookie and rotating around so that she was facing the backseat, "I'm pretty annoyed with all the new rules Petra insisted on. I mean, cheek kisses only? It's *so* fifth grade."

"Yeah, and having a table between us," Johnny added. "Guess they don't want everyone feeling each other up. Which is probably a good thing. I don't want to be molested by some weirdo who can't keep her claws off me."

I laughed. I couldn't help it. The idea of that happening was just so random.

"There's a lot you can do, even with a 'no-hands' policy," Bella pointed out, wiggling her eyebrows at no one in particular.

I snorted. "Well, anyway, the idea is still really cute, but we have to market it right," I said, trying to channel my dad's advertising prowess. "For one thing," I continued, "we have to create a lot of initial buzz so people know to look out for the booth. Then we also have to make our booth appealing to as wide a variety of people as possible. It can't just be some folding table with a sign over it."

Bella had gotten out her notebook and was jotting down everything I said. She looked up suddenly. "Something I just realized is, if we're going to have at least one guy and one girl in the booth at all times, then Johnny and Dan are going to have to do way more shifts than the rest of us." She turned to Johnny. "Think you're up to the task?"

Johnny pretended to loosen his collar. "Hey, I'm used to being in high demand, what can I say."

Then Bella swiveled toward the backseat again. "And what about you, Lis? Are you, um, *prepared* for the, you know, the actual kissing part?"

My cheeks heated up again. Bella had a nefarious glint in her eye. Kind of like how she looked at Apples & Oranges the other day — like she was trying to call me out. But why? It was times like these that I would kill to have Mo around. Mo who was now buddies with the Fly Girls. It seemed like everything in my life was just slightly *off* these days, and I didn't know how to get things back on track.

"Yeah," I answered Bella, trying to sound unfazed. "It's cool."

"Because," Bella went on, still wearing that strange expression, "if you *are* nervous — and I could understand why you would be — then maybe you should, like, get some practice. I mean I'm sure you could just practice on Rothberg here," she said, punching Johnny's shoulder. "He won't mind."

"What?!" I felt myself jolt upward.

"Whoa!" Bella told Johnny, "Calm down, cowboy, you totally just drove onto the curve."

"Sorry," Johnny muttered. "Listen, I think we've done enough planning for now. We're probably going to miss the second bell."

Chapter 10

"We're talking dead corpse — I mean, there's no such thing as a live corpse. Well, unless it's a zombie — yes, actually, a zombie, that is the perfect analogy!" Bella shouted a bit too loudly. An older couple in line near us turned to see what was going on.

Bella went on obliviously. "Like, Pete sticks his tongue in my mouth, and then, *lah* . . . it's just sitting there not moving. Like, what do I do with this?" she said, waving her arms around. "Excuse me, I thought we were supposed to be kissing, but I guess he was just trying to turn me into a bride of the undead or whatever."

"Gross! Really? Pete Simmons?" I fiddled with the latch on the white purse I'd taken from Claire's closet earlier. "Pete is now part of The Plan?" I felt a little — okay a lot — behind. I was too preoccupied with my own thoughts. Why had Brett and Jackie broken up? Who had dumped who? And why had Mo been hanging with the Fly Girls ever since? Was it all connected somehow? I just couldn't fit it all together in my mind.

Bella stared at me. "Lisi. When are you going to get it through your head? I am willing to do *anything* here. Practically."

"It's just, he's the fourth guy you've kissed since the New Year."

"Yes, but he was only step two in The Plan, after Jeff. You have to look at it that way." The big round bulbs over the movie kiosk made Bella's expression look particularly devious.

"Oh. Well, did it work? Did Mason react?" I spread some lip gloss on my lips and looked for Johnny.

"That's the thing. We were right near Mason's locker during passing period. He couldn't have missed it."

"In the *hall*?" Since when had Bella become one of those girls who made out with people in the hallways?

"Oh, Lisi. It's so cute how naïve you are," Bella said, as Johnny joined us balancing his camera (as always) as well as a big carton of popcorn, Milk Duds, and a large Coke with three straws poking out of it.

"I know you guys are skeptical, but you are really going to like this," he said, nodding toward the movie we were waiting in line for. It was the latest Luc Martinez–directed film and Johnny had been reading up on it for months.

The Northside Loews always had long lines outside the theaters. My theory was that the staff was just too disgruntled to clean the theaters fast enough, so even unpopular movies like the one we were about to watch still had lines for them. It would have been annoying, except that now it had become sort of a known *thing*. Anyone from NHS had a good chance of running into someone else they wanted to see from NHS while waiting in these lines. In a strange way, it had become the place to see and be seen.

"Isn't it in subtitles?" I asked, taking the carton of popcorn from him and nibbling on a top piece that was covered in butter and salt.

"Yeah, but I hear the cinematography is totally innovative, and all the reviews say it's really visceral. It's not so much about war, it's about the definition of survival."

Bella groaned. "I wish Luc was *in* the movie. That might be something worth watching."

"What, would you guys rather be watching *that*?" Johnny asked, pointing to the sign for the new Adam Brody movie. He said the word *that* like it was toxic. Bella and I glanced at the poster — a picture of Adam Brody standing with his hands in his jeans pockets, looking adorable — and then back at each other. I knew what was going through both our heads: of course we'd rather see *So They Call This Love*. But since Johnny was our official chauffeur, and since he knew the most about film, it was the unstated rule that if there was something he really wanted to see, we'd let him choose. We had all seen some pretty interesting movies because of this policy, though often Bella, Mo, and I would return to one of our houses afterward and pop in a DVD like *13 Going on 30*, just to cleanse the palate.

"'Scuse me," a girl with stick-straight blond hair said behind us. "Is this the line for *Brother Sword*?"

"Why, *yes*," Johnny stated dramatically and gestured toward the line. "Welcome to an experience you are never going to forget," he intoned, quoting the trailer. The girl giggled. She had two friends standing behind her, and they all seemed vaguely familiar. They were probably freshmen girls. They had that look. And it was a Friday night in Northside. Pretty much the only thing to do was go to the movies.

An interesting thing happened then. It started when the frosh girls began talking about their plans for Spring Carnival. I was throwing popcorn at Johnny's face and he was trying to catch it with his mouth, so for a second we didn't notice when Bella, inevitably, piped into the frosh girls' conversation.

I tuned in when I heard Bella saying, "Oh, that would be such a tremendous help to us. Here, have some Milk Duds." Bella opened the box and dumped a bunch of Milk Duds into the girls' hands.

"What are they helping with?" Johnny asked, turning around. As he did so, the piece of popcorn I had just launched hit him in the chest and fell to the ground.

"Johnny!" Bella said with a big smile. "This is Trish. She and her friends want to help us with our kissing booth campaign."

I smirked and whispered to Johnny, "Maybe it should be called the kiss-up booth instead."

If he heard me, he didn't show it. He stuffed his hands into his pockets, Adam Brody style.

"We're really good at posters," Trish said. Her friends still stood behind her and shifted their weight back and forth. I noticed they were all wearing heels. To the movies. Totally trying too hard. Definitely freshmen. I briefly wondered if Bella and Mo and I had looked like that two years ago. Probably. Or maybe not.

"Good at posters, huh?" Johnny stared at Trish. "Important skill to have." He sounded so serious that the girls couldn't seem to tell if he was being sarcastic or not. Come to think of it, I couldn't tell either.

He held up his mini DVD cam. "Mind if I turn this on for a sec?" he asked. Often when he was roaming the halls at school, he would leave the camera on, but he usually held it at his chest, not his eye, so it wasn't that obvious that he was filming. But for some reason, doing it at the movie theater seemed particularly embarrassing.

Bella ignored him. "Great. Can you meet me by the flag next Monday? I'll give you instructions then."

Trish leaned in closer to Johnny. "Are you going to be there, too?" she asked him.

I could see the color rising in Johnny's neck as he switched his camera off. The girl was completely coming on to him, right there in the Loews Cineplex lobby! Johnny did have a slightly hip look. I could maybe see why a girl like Trish would flirt with him. But did she have to be so *obvious* about it? Yeesh.

The moment was so awkward I had to pretend I wasn't there with them. Instead I glanced around the movie theater idly, and that's when I saw her.

"Mo!"

Or at least, it looked a lot like Mo. All I really saw through the crowd was a poof of blond hair and what appeared to be a hand carrying Twizzlers. Definitely Mo. Then right near her, I caught sight of Cindy Ramirez, one of the girls from the dance team. So it was for real. Mo was friends with *those girls* now. She was even going to the movies with them — something that had been *our* tradition since forever. Suddenly, just because she got a makeover, she didn't need us anymore? How had this happened?

"I'll be right back," I said quickly and thrust the popcorn back into Johnny's arms as I darted toward the cardboard cutout of Will Smith I'd seen Mo approach.

"Maybe she just wants to be left alone," I heard Johnny call after me as I scurried away. Why would she want to be left alone? I had to talk to her. Something was seriously wrong, I just knew it. And I had to find out if Mo had said anything about my crush on Brett!

But by the time I had woven my way across the lobby, I couldn't tell where Mo had gone. Turning around in a circle, I spotted the *So They Call This Love* entrance and made my way toward it. Then I felt a hand on my arm.

"Ticket, miss?" asked the scrawny, pimply ticket collector. He looked about my age, but I didn't recognize him. He probably went to the private school in the town over. Probably had too many pimples to handle public school.

"I'm just looking for someone," I pleaded.

The ticket kid grinned an ugly grin. "Can't go in without a ticket. Sorry." Then he leaned around me and tore someone else's ticket to let them go by.

I gave one more search with no luck and then gave up and headed back to the *Brother Sword* line. By the time I got there, the line had started moving and Bella and Johnny were almost near the entrance. I jogged over to join them, feeling confused and sad.

I guess ever since we saw Mo at lunch with Jackie yesterday, I had been hoping that it was just some strange circumstance, like Mo just happened to sit at the wrong table, right as we were walking in. I kept believing, as she avoided my calls, texts, and IMs last night that she was just really busy working on a project for school. I had had enough to distract me with the kissing booth plans that it hadn't been that hard to pretend.

But who was I kidding. Mo was angry with us. And she didn't want to tell us why.

When I approached Johnny and Bella again, Bella was back to begging Johnny to show her the footage of the Mason and Brett interview.

Johnny looked annoyed. "Bella, ask Lisi. She gets it."

"I get what?"

"Why it's uncool to show the interview of Mason Firestone and Brett Jacobson prematurely," he said, his eyes intense.

I almost agreed with him, but then I paused for a second. Brett and Jacqueline had broken up. And no one knew why.

Except, maybe, Johnny. And his camera. Johnny had been known to get the truth out of people like no one else could. That's what made him so great at what he did. And that's what made Bella so desperate to see the footage of Mason. And maybe that's what was causing Johnny's eyes to sparkle with determination — and secrets.

"You know," I hedged. "I don't see how it could be *that* bad to just give us a sneak preview. I mean, you don't have to be so self-conscious about your work," I added.

But Johnny snorted in disgust and refused to answer. Instead he turned around and handed our three tickets to the ticket collector (less pimply and also friendlier than the one on the other side of the lobby) and marched ahead to find the best seats.

Bella turned to me. "Well, thanks for trying," she said, clearly assuming I had only piped up because I wanted to help her with Plan Mason Seduction. She leaned to the side and nudged my arm with her shoulder. "But I'll figure out a way. Don't worry."

Chapter 11

Saturday, 10p.m.

R U COMING OVR?

I hit SEND and waited a few seconds. Then I opened up a new text and typed:

BELLA HAS TOTS.

Ever since we'd rented *Napoleon Dynamite* at Mo's High School Sucks themed birthday party at the end of eighth grade, we had become obsessed with eating Tater Tots like Napoleon does in the movie. I was trying anything at this point to get Molly to text me back. I stared at my phone's blank screen. Finally I typed one last text:

WE MISS U!!!!

Then I placed my phone on the shiny black coffee table in Lucy Haverman's totally mod living room and returned to my *Teen Vogue*, settling back into the cushions of the big steel-gray leather couch. Bella had subscriptions to all the good magazines: *Seventeen, Teen Vogue, CosmoGirl,* and *Marie Claire.* She would let me have them only after she'd had a chance to read the whole thing herself, because she knew I always cut them up to make collages, rendering the articles completely unreadable.

We were having our Saturday night sleepover. We almost always had sleepovers on Saturdays because it was Lucy's date night and there was nothing Bella hated more than to be left alone on a Saturday night. Sometimes just Mo came over, sometimes just me, but usually it was all three of us. Of course, tonight it was just me and Bella, the way it had been all week since spring break — ever since Molly's new "look."

And Mo had been avoiding Johnny, too. He said he hadn't really talked with her since Tuesday. All he'd said about the matter was that he'd gotten the sense she just "needed some space." But who needed space from their best friends? Especially when everything had seemed so normal with her that first evening back?

"Wait!" Bella said, getting up onto her knees from her spot on the plush-carpeted floor. "Don't cut into the Jake Gyllenhaal article until you read the whole thing. At the end he says all this great stuff about getting his heart ripped out and stomped all over. *So* sexy."

I put down my scissors and sighed. We had spent the last couple hours raiding the freezer for Tater Tots and other frozen snacks, and digging into Bella's pile of magazines that had all arrived over spring break. It was all fun, but.

"Doesn't it just kind of depress you?" I asked.

"What, the fact that Jake will never in a million years be mine? Of course! But every girl needs a healthy dose of humility. Or so I hear," Bella said, dog-earring a page in *Marie Claire* with a picture of a girl in a shiny turquoise party dress. She held it up. "Truth. Would I look like a sapphire goddess or, like, a blueberry?"

I grabbed the page. "You'd look like you were completely broke. This dress is seven hundred and ninety-nine dollars. Anyway, I wasn't talking about Jake, even though, yes, his aloofness *is* devastating. I meant the whole Mo situation."

Bella sighed. "I know. It makes me really mad that she would just ditch us all of a sudden with no explanation. But on the other hand," she said, looking down at her pile of magazines, "when someone needs space, they need space. It's really not our place to judge. At least that's what my mother always says to justify the jerks who date her for a couple months and then disappear into the ether. People sometimes need space, yada yada. I'm not saying I get it, but I'm just saying it's not the first time in the universe that someone who you *think* is always going to be there for you just evaporates like snow." Bella was twisting her hair around one of her hands, still staring at the magazines.

"I'm pretty sure snow doesn't just evaporate really. It melts into puddles and then the water evaporates."

"Oh, don't be such a know-it-all," Bella laughed, and threw the June *Seventeen* at me. I laughed and grabbed the *Teen Vogue* with the Jake Gyllenhaal article. I tore the pages out of the magazine in a big chunk and started tearing them into confetti with what I knew must be a wickedly goofy look on my face.

"Ah!" Bella gasped dramatically. She ripped the picture of the blue dress out of the *Marie Claire* and shredded it to pieces over my head. She started cracking up when a piece fell down my shirt and I started hopping around, trying to shake it out. Pretty soon, we were grabbing any pages we could and crumpling, ripping, and throwing them everywhere. It was kind of hilarious. I couldn't stop laughing hysterically.

"Okay, seriously, seriously!" Bella giggled, trying to call a truce. "Lucy is going to *murder* us." She surveyed the mess. "Maybe we should call Sasha."

"The maid? Now? On a Saturday night? Who does that?"

"I do!" Bella shrugged and smiled.

"No, no, we can just grab the DustBuster, come on." I ran down the wide front hallway to the storage closet toward the back of the house, the one that contained all the housekeeping supplies. This wasn't the first time we'd had to do damage control before Lucy got home.

When I came back to the living room, Bella had managed to pick up all the large pieces of magazine paper, and I easily sucked up the rest with the Dust-Buster. "Good job, buddy," I said, patting the DustBuster as I headed back to put it away.

"Hey," Bella called, following me down the hall. "I know what will cheer you up. Our DVD for tonight."

"Is Jake in it?"

"No, even *better*. It's a surprise."

I grabbed sodas for both of us from the fridge and met Bella in the den.

"What's this amazing DVD we're going to watch?" I asked. "If it's not Jake, who is it? Adam Brody? Orlando?"

Bella was standing in the room with something hidden behind her back. She smiled mysteriously. "Like I said, better." She inched over to the flat screen and slid the DVD into the player.

"Give me a hint," I said as Bella joined me on the cushy fawn-colored couch.

"Johnny."

"Johnny Depp? *Pirates of the Caribbean*?"

"Rothberg."

"What?" I grabbed the remote out of Bella's hand. "*Our* Johnny? Wait, Bella, wait. Did he give you his film? How did you convince him? When did this happen? Last night he was freaking out about how he didn't want us watching it."

Bella said nothing; she just looked smugly at the screen.

"Bella . . . you didn't. Oh my God. Seriously. *Please*

tell me you did not steal it from his car. *Please* tell me you didn't do it. He will die. Or we will die."

"Whatever! He's being so lame and squeamish about it! I have an agenda! As my friend, he should be more willing to help me out. He's so absorbed in his artsy-fartsy film head all the time it's like what the rest of us want doesn't matter."

"Bella, that's because this film is, like, the most important thing to him in the world."

"More important than us?" Bella asked. I was silent. Truthfully, I wasn't sure. Johnny was great. He was probably the most reliable person I knew — way more reliable than Bella. And after all that had happened this week, he was definitely more reliable than Mo. But he *loved* film. He was obsessed with it. Maybe even more so than I was with Brett, or Bella claimed to be with Mason.

"Well," I sighed. "What's done is done." I thought about the secrets I was on the brink of discovering about Brett. It made me a little nervous. But part of me, this part I didn't really want to admit, was more excited than I had been in a long time.

"But we swear to get this back to him before he even notices it's missing. I'll slip it into his car on the way to school Monday, and with any luck, he'll never know we had it. Deal?"

"Deal," Bella said, taking the remote back and pressing PLAY.

We both eagerly leaned forward.

The DVD opened up with some footage of the NHS hallways and the front circle. People passed by, oblivious to the fact that the camera was there. This guy Judson Green stuck an M&M up his nose. I was enthralled. It was hard to explain why this was so cool to watch. For one thing, it was like seeing life through Johnny's eyes. And even in its unedited version, it just felt so . . . professional. I finally understood what Johnny had meant all this time about wanting his film to show what high school was *really* like.

We watched as an interview with Sarah Singer in the cafeteria began. She was eating a yogurt and explaining how she wanted to start her own business someday, selling soap. It was kind of funny, but also sad, the way the cam zoomed in on her face when she said the word "soap." Maybe it was the angles, or the intimacy of the moments Johnny had picked up on his Minicam, but it finally clicked that Johnny had real skill to match his passion. Sure, I'd seen plenty of snippets of his work before — him filming his little brothers and parents around the house, the neighborhood kids, and a couple of comedy sketches he'd done in middle school. But this was different. There was something really smart and mature about it. I couldn't believe it, but I was riveted.

And looking over at Bella, I could tell she was, too.

The camera cut to a curbside, not far from the school. I recognized where it was because you could see the corner of the Store24 in the background. I swallowed hard. This was it, we were about to see an interview with Brett — and Mason — and find out their secrets! It had to be — Johnny had said they were the last people he'd interviewed.

I was so tense I was hardly breathing. Would Brett admit the reasons for his and Jacqueline's breakup? Would he say there was another girl in his life? Would there be any clue I could take and use somehow — learn some way to at least lure Brett to the kissing booth?

But instead of the face of the boy I had daydreamed about for the past two and a half years, Mo's face filled the camera. She was sitting on the curb.

"Oh," Bella breathed. "Maybe this is the wrong disk. Great."

But just as Bella started complaining, Mo started talking on the screen. And what she said chilled me to the bone.

Mo was leaning with one hand on the sidewalk and her legs in her new tight jeans stretched into the street. She swayed her tall boots from side to side. She looked so . . . *pretty.*

"What do I see as the purpose of high school?" she murmured, apparently mulling over the question. She was squinting a little and looking across the street.

Then she turned to face the camera and it felt like she was looking straight at me and Bella as she said confidently, "High school is the time to broaden your horizons. To discover who you are, what you really want from life. Sometimes that's not easy because your friends want you to stay the same forever." Bella and I gaped at the screen. She went on, "But if you don't climb the social ladder now, you could miss your chance."

I heard Johnny's voice in the background asking a question, but I was still reeling from what Mo had just said. *Broaden your horizons?* What was she, a brochure? *Your friends want you to stay the same forever* — was she talking about us? Then Mo sat up a little straighter and dusted her hand off on the side of her jeans.

"I'm sick of the status quo. The status quo is me constantly getting stepped on by my so-called best friends. They think they know everything about me, but actually they don't notice *anything*. And that's not friendship. That's basically just the definition of self-ishness." She twirled one of her crazy blond kinks. "So, yeah. That's what I think. It gets cold being in the shadow of people like Lisi and Bella, you know what I mean?"

Johnny muttered something, and then Mo said, "Hey, can I tell you something off the record?" Then the camera switched off.

The screen went dark.

And we were left staring at it in complete horror. I felt like my heart had just dropped into my stomach. Like I'd fallen on my back and gotten the wind knocked out of me. That's how shocked I was.

In all of my years of friendship with Mo, she had *never* said anything as hurtful to me as the words she'd just spoken. Well, she wasn't saying the words to me, at least not directly. Which made it even worse. She'd told *someone else*. That was another thing. Whenever something was bothering Mo, she always turned to me. Well, she always *had* anyway. Apparently not anymore.

Apparently she thought Bella and I were just selfish mean girls who no longer deserved to be friends with her.

"That little . . ." Bella muttered, with a calmness that scared me more than her normal melodrama. "I can't believe her."

"I know."

"I don't even know what to say!"

"I know."

"Who the hell does she think she is anyway?"

"I don't know."

"Jacqueline has poisoned Mo against us. There's no other explanation for it. For whatever reason, Jacqueline decided to be friends with Mo and turn her against us. It's the only way I can figure it out."

"You think?" I asked, suddenly worried. "Why would Jacqueline do that? Why would she care in the first place?"

Bella looked at me with confusion that mirrored my own.

"I am so angry I could SCREAM!" she suddenly shouted, throwing the remote down onto the black coffee table with so much force that the back fell off and the batteries flew out.

We sat there listening to them roll away along the shiny hardwood floor of the den. Then Bella got up off the couch and darted out of the room.

"Bella, where are you going?"

In a minute she stomped back in with her laptop in one hand, plopped down, and flung it open. She immediately logged onto her e-mail and started typing furiously.

"Whoa, whoa, are you e-mailing Mo? Maybe we should calm down for a minute and try to think about this situation more."

"What's there to think about?" Bella asked. "No one has the right to treat us this way. It's time you learned to stand up for yourself for once."

I chose to ignore the dig. I knew Bella was just spewing because she was insulted — and hurt.

"But, Bella," I said as she continued to type, "Mo and Johnny don't know we watched the DVD, remember? They don't know we know. And if we tell them, we have to admit how we got it. And you know how Johnny will get. Do we really want *him* turning against us, too?" I asked, seriously afraid now of what we'd gotten ourselves into.

Bella paused.

"You're right," she said. I saw her click SAVE on the draft of her e-mail and close the window. "You're right, we can't let Johnny find out how we know. God. This is just so unfair."

I refrained from pointing out that stealing his DVD was also not exactly fair. Now was clearly not the time.

"It's worse than I thought," Bella continued. "She's not just done with us. It's so much worse than we thought."

"What do you mean?" I asked, feeling my throat constrict. How could there be anything worse than your best friend and the person you trusted most in the world, like family, suddenly being "done" with you?

"What I mean is, she resented us all along. Our friendship as we knew it was a lie. All this time, she was secretly seething, just waiting to hit a boiling point. And there's nothing we could even do about it. Because we didn't know. All this time, we didn't know how she felt."

Bella shook her head slowly. I blinked back tears. I felt like someone had died, like some part of *me* had died. Or some part of my childhood. My head ached and suddenly I couldn't think about anything except needing to lie down.

"Wanna watch a Will Ferrell movie or something? Try to lift the mood a little?" Bella asked.

I shrugged. I couldn't bring myself to say anything more.

Maybe Bella slipped in a new movie. Maybe she didn't. I stared at the TV, but I didn't see anything. Except Mo's face, her voice, in a tone I wasn't used to, saying "it gets cold," over and over again in my mind.

I shivered and huddled deeper into the noisy leather couch in Bella's den.

Mo and I had played together when we were *babies*. Way before I was friends with Bella or even Johnny. And then, just like that, the rug had been pulled out from under the friendship, while I was looking the other way.

All week it had been obvious something was off.

I suddenly realized that maybe if I hadn't been so caught up in my secret plans for kissing Brett at the kissing booth, I might have noticed something had gone terribly wrong with Mo.

Something way beyond simply eating at a new lunch table or seeing movies with the Fly Girls. Something *really* wrong.

But now, apparently, it was too late.

Chapter 12

Sunday, 12 p.m.

"Dum dum dadada dum da dum."

I turned up the volume on my computer speakers, hoping Ingrid Michaelson would drown out the sound of my dad humming to himself while he read the Sunday paper downstairs. My dad is a big guy, almost six foot three, so his voice really carries, and he is always humming the melodies to commercials that have the annoying tendency to stick in one's head forever. This morning it sounded distinctly like the Charmin toilet paper theme song.

I shoved the stack of magazines I had brought home from Bella's house off of my bed, and they fell in a messy heap on the floor. I stared at the ceiling. If only I could be like Bella, and just be angry about it all. That would be so much easier. Easier than the way I really felt, which was . . . awful.

Maybe I had a fever.

I supposed in a way that this was poetic justice — it's what we deserved for stealing Johnny's DVD in the first place. And that was a whole other ball of wax I had to worry about — if he found out, he'd be so upset. It wasn't just about the DVD. It was the fact that we had blatantly disrespected the thing that was so important to him. That gnawed at me, too.

But that was minor compared to the real issue at hand. Mo. Molly. Our former best friend. It was just so unbelievable.

I replayed for the millionth time what had happened last night in Bella's den, and thought, *I wouldn't even want to be friends with myself.*

First, I had a secret from almost all of my friends. Second, I had offered to help Bella get Mason but really I was just trying to serve my own plan of getting Brett to kiss me at Spring Carnival. Third, I had sided with Bella and betrayed Johnny's trust. Fourth, I had tried to find out personal stuff about Brett, which did, when you really thought about it, make the whole thing kind of, well, stalkerish.

It was no wonder Mo didn't want us to be friends anymore.

But that didn't make it sting any less.

I woke a few hours later to a soft knocking on my bedroom door.

"Lisi, honey?" My mom poked her head into the room. "Were you napping?"

I nodded groggily, removing my huge Pooh Bear pillow from my face. "What time's it?"

"About three o'clock. Is everything okay? You've been moping around a lot more than usual," my mom observed, sitting down on the foot of the bed.

How could I tell my mom about Mo, when it still hardly made any sense to me? Besides, Mom was best friends with Mo's mom. She'd just tell me to go over and apologize.

But how do you apologize for your personality? If you are, inherently, a bad person and a bad friend?

Instead I just shrugged. "Didn't get much sleep at Bella's," I said, by way of explanation.

My mother seemed to accept that. "Well, it's a beautiful day out. Now that you've had a nap, why don't you join me and your father downtown for the Farmers Market?"

Every month from April to October, there's a market downtown where people from farms up to an hour or two away gather to sell their products for exorbitant prices. And they get away with it, too, partly because there isn't a Whole Foods anywhere nearby, or any other way for health nuts to get their fix of overpriced and mini-size vegetables and fruits, not to mention bizarre-looking "handwoven" clothing. My mom loves all the local crafts and flowers and things. And Dad is mildly obsessed with organic food, ever since he'd bonded with Ashlee Simpson at a Skechers commercial shoot.

Apparently, in her spare time, Ashlee is a crusader against pesticides.

Basically, it sounded like the most boring thing I could think of. "*Moooooom*," I whined.

"You don't get enough fresh air. Come on, Lis, it'll be nice." My mom pulled the comforter off of me and ruffled my hair, which I really hate. She knew how sensitive I was about my short hair.

"Okay, okay, I'll go with you, just stop messing up my hair. It's fragile!"

I threw on a clean pair of jeans and met my parents downstairs. The car was quiet as we drove to the market, except for Dad's humming.

We meandered around the main tent for a while, my father rattling on about plant parasites, heirloom produce, and other stuff I knew nothing about. My mom got into the "zone" where I could tell she was plotting a painting in her mind. My dad bought us ice creams. I ordered pistachio, though I wasn't really hungry.

It was all very quaint, predictable, and generally pointless, the way an afternoon with the family is supposed to feel. It was a nice hiatus from reality, in a way.

If Claire had been around, the two of us would have gone off to some of the cooler jewelry stands or wandered on our own. But as it was, I was stuck with just my parents, which made me feel like a little kid.

Not necessarily a bad thing.

That is, until someone ran into me and sent my pistachio ice cream careening into the spot on my chest where boobs would be if I had boobs. The ice cream left a pale green sticky smear like alien goo across my pink tube top. Correction: *Claire's* pink tube top.

Equally embarrassing was the awkward way I screeched "Whoa!!!!" as it was happening and staggered slightly.

But I realized all of that was nothing compared to the humiliation of looking up into Brett's startled silver-blue eyes. Again. What was his deal with crashing into me? Was I really THAT invisible? And was he going to actually try to talk to me now?

"Oh, oh man. My bad. I'm so sorry, Lisa."

I was so surprised I just gaped.

"Lisa?"

"Lisi," I managed.

"What?"

"It's Lisi."

"Right. Sorry, Lisi. Totally didn't see you." Of course he didn't see me. He never saw me. Not really. And I saw him everywhere.

He flipped his light brown hair out of his eyes. "Can I, like, get you a new one or something?" he asked, gesturing with his chin to the rest of the cone, which was lying on the ground.

I glanced around. My parents had continued walking by the fountain in the center square, already several yards away, caught up in their own worlds as usual. No one, in fact, was paying any attention to me and Brett. No one else around seemed to realize the intensity of the moment. It was literally the first time I had *ever* had a private conversation with Brett.

If you could call it a conversation.

"Um, I mean, sure," I stammered. The green mark on my shirt seemed to be drying into a dark blob. Maybe it looked like part of the design?

Nope, it pretty much just looked like melted pistachio ice cream.

Brett turned around and headed for the organic ice cream stand. I figured I didn't really have much choice but to follow him, so I hurried along at his side but slightly behind him, in case he didn't want it to seem like we were actually going somewhere together.

Were we? Going somewhere together? Did this count?

I couldn't really think of anything else to say until we got to the ice-cream counter and he asked me what flavor I wanted. It was so out of the ordinary that this guy I had imagined talking to so many times was actually speaking to me in *real life*, it took me a second to realize I was supposed to, like, respond.

"Green. I mean, um, pistachio. Thanks!" Was it just me or did my voice sound like someone had told me I'd just won the lottery?

I grabbed some napkins and dabbed at Claire's pink tube top while he ordered. Slightly better. At least I didn't look as though I'd gotten slimed like the ghost-busters anymore. (Johnny had made me watch the *Ghostbusters* movies one Sunday last year. I strangely wished I was at his house again, at least for a second, where I could feel like myself.)

But there I was, clutching a whole new ice cream cone and standing about a foot apart from Brett Jacobson, having no idea in the world what to do next.

And he didn't seem to be going anywhere. In fact, he was talking to me still! "So, like, what exactly is pistachio? I've always wondered that."

How could you not know what pistachio is? "Nuts. I mean, it's, um, a kind of nut." Well, so much for flowing convo.

"Ah," he said, with a slight smile. Did he think I was trying to be funny? Well, that was better at least than his realizing I was actually just a stammering fool. I didn't want that semi-smile to disappear. Not yet.

"So," I said, stalling. *Just pretend you're talking to someone normal, like Johnny.* "What are you doing here? This is officially Northside's lamest attempt at community togetherness, don't you think?" I asked, hoping he was on the brink of discovering just how witty, smart, and fun I could be.

Yeah, I'm a regular comedian. They should pay me for my hilarious one-liners.

He squinted into the sun. "That's my dad's," he said, pointing at a fancy antique furniture retailer.

Oops.

"The one with the yellow flag over it, yeah, that one." He was pointing to one of the poshest-looking stands on the street.

"Oh. That's, um. Really nice. I like it." *I like it?*

"Yup. My dad's one true love. Antique and rare collectibles trading."

"Cool," I said, nervously staring at my ice cream. I didn't want it to melt all over my arm, but I wasn't sure I wanted to risk actually trying to lick the cone in front of Brett.

"Not really."

"What?"

"It's not really that cool. I mean, whatever, he loves his collecting and trading, I get that, that's fine, ya know? But it's all about investing in the future, always exchanging what you have for the better deal, the most valuable item on the market. It's like this metaphor. He wants me to learn to invest, too."

"That sounds really . . . fun," I said, still kind of perplexed as to why Brett was still standing next to me. Apparently he didn't have anything better to do. Which meant we actually had something in common.

I was trying to think of some way to mention Spring Carnival, but Brett cut into my thoughts.

"Whatever. My father is the total cliché of the perfectionist high-pressure parent who thinks things like where I go to college and what grade I get on every single assignment is of utmost importance. As if our high school grades will ever matter in the real world. I guess this day is just all about him, and it would be like the end of the known world if I didn't care deeply about all of it."

Whoa.

Could we possibly be any more soul-mate-ish? Granted, I didn't have an overbearing father, or a pressure to make financial investments, or any idea really about what colleges I would apply to.

But I felt like I *got* Brett in this moment. He was stressed. His life wasn't perfect. On the one hand, this seemed obvious — no one's life was perfect. But, for some reason with Brett, it just made me realize that he had a lot of depth, and he was finally letting me see some of it. Willingly. Like, I didn't have to piece together his inner thoughts and struggles by reading his newspaper articles. He was just *telling* me his deepest feelings about life.

"Anyway, sorry to vent at you." He turned to face me and for a moment he held my eyes with his. He trusted me.

My heart felt like it was going to burst out of my chest and blow away in the gentle spring breeze. In a good way.

And then, my heart went from beating really quickly to practically stopping beating altogether as he leaned toward me.

My body froze.

Then he whispered, "Careful."

I looked down and saw he was referring to the ice cream that was beginning to drip down my hand.

Or was he?

He turned to leave and I watched him move away, the flowing fountain in the square sparkling a hundred shades of blue and silver.

Chapter 13

Monday, 12p.m.

Chicken fingers! Maybe that was a good omen. The caf almost never served anything as delicious as chicken fingers, and I almost never brought money for lunch. But my mom was so far into the crazy zone of preparing for her big show that she didn't have time that morning to throw a few slices of turkey on limp bread. Things were looking up.

I carried my tray toward the table where Bella and Johnny were already sitting. Bella had a salad and seltzer in front of her, as always, but she was eating Johnny's french fries. Also a great sign. That meant everyone was still friends and no one was mad at each other.

Which in turn meant that when I had subtly "found" Johnny's DVD on the floor of his car that morning on our way to school, he really hadn't noticed that it had actually come out of the front pocket of my backpack. He *did* have a major look of concern on his face, but all he'd said was, "Oh man, so glad you found that. I thought I'd lost it somewhere." So he didn't know Bella had taken it.

And he didn't have to.

I glanced around the caf as I headed to our table, and I didn't spot Mo among the many faces. But just as I set my tray down next to Johnny's — in fact, right as Bella was saying, "Do I get a bite?" and reaching for one of the chicken fingers, a loud sound shook the cafeteria.

"HEY HEY, YOU YOU!"

It was the opening of Avril Lavigne's "Girlfriend," and it was blaring out of an iPod boom box carried in on Cindy Ramirez's shoulder. The rest of the Fly Girls came running in from behind her and started fanning out down the aisles of the caf, doing choreographed moves to the song. It was like a scene from *Bring It On*. There were twelve girls on the team but somehow, the way they were taking over the caf and running around, it seemed like there were fifty of them. It was kind of cool, actually. Some people were rolling their eyes, but most of the caf was into it, laughing, clapping, or shouting. Brian DeLancy stood up and demanded a lap dance but everyone ignored him and he sat down pretty quickly — probably fearing another chocolate milk incident.

Toward the end of their dance, the girls cleared off a table and Jacqueline leaped onto it. I noticed Brett watching Jacqueline closely, his expression unreadable.

As the song died down, Mo appeared beside the table. She and another girl held either end of a long poster that said DANCE DANCE REVOLUTION DANCE-OFF! The music ended and Jacqueline addressed her audience.

"Hey, guys! Me and the Fly Girls just wanted to make a quick announcement, 'kay? First of all, I want to ask you *all* to join in our dance-off at Spring Carnival. It's going to rock!"

A bunch of the Fly Girls shouted "Woooh!" and "Yeah!"

"Anyways, anyways," Jacqueline continued, laughing and adjusting her miniature skirt, which clearly wasn't designed for standing on tables in. Or maybe that's exactly what it was designed for.

"If our booth wins the prize this year, I'll be having my graduation bash in a club in New York City!" More shouts of excitement from her cronies. "And anyone who buys a ticket to our booth is invited! That's all!"

She hopped off the table, and the cafeteria exploded into excited murmurs.

Bella dropped the chicken finger back onto my plate. "I just lost my appetite."

*   *   *

"This?" Johnny asked incredulously later that afternoon, pointing to a big yellow poster board hanging by the door to the gym. It said KISSING BOOTH diagonally across it with glitter framing the whole thing like a giant sparkling lemon bar. There was another one like it outside the door to the library and one on the door to the auditorium. "This is what that chick meant by 'I'm good at posters'?" he said, imitating the girl we'd met at the movie theater in a really girly voice that kind of made me want to laugh. But his point was serious.

"Bella, I hate to agree, but there is just no *way* we are going to compete with the Fly Girls." I shifted the weight of my backpack.

"I am so mad I could scream!" Bella said, grabbing her hairbrush from the front pocket of her bag and brushing her shiny hair furiously. "I could kill that girl."

"Who, Trish?" I dropped my bag on the ground. The thing weighed a ton. "She's only a freshman. She doesn't know any better. She certainly didn't know Jacqueline was going to put up such a fight. I mean, *we* didn't see that coming either." Usually the dance team, the basketball team's dunking booth, and the student council's pie-throwing booth were the main contenders for winning the prize. But none had ever made such an overt attempt to win. I guess there'd never been such a big prize before.

"No," Bella said, pausing her frantic brushstrokes. "Not Trish. Mo. I am going to kill Mo. Mo who was supposed to be on *our* side and is now holding up banners for the Fly Girls. Mo who knew how much we wanted to win this thing."

"You really think she and Jacqueline want to squash us on purpose?" I asked, not quite sure where Bella was going with this.

"This means war," Bella said, her eyes glinting.

I tried to widen my eyes at Bella to warn her not to say too much. *Remember, Johnny doesn't know that we know that Mo hates us. He doesn't know we watched the interview,* I tried to convey via ESP.

Maybe it worked, because Bella huffed loudly. "I'm going to find Trish. We'll do some damage control. We'll figure this out. It's all about the incentive."

"Incentive?" Johnny asked, warily.

"Well, yeah," Bella said. "Jacqueline pretty much bribed the entire school by saying they can come to her big ridiculous party if they buy a ticket."

"Yeah, but we're not graduating yet, and we're not having a big wild party, and even if we were, no one would give a monkey's butt," Johnny said, frustrated.

"We have to think of *something*," Bella insisted. "Okay, I'm finding Trish and the crew. We'll reconvene on this tomorrow." She marched off in the direction of the stairwell.

Johnny and I stared at each other. "Are you thinking what I'm thinking?" he asked.

"That it's always scary when Bella says she'll 'think of something'?"

"Exactly."

A few guys in gym clothes swung the door open and passed between us, high-fiving each other. They smelled like sweat.

After they were gone, Johnny stepped away from the door. "So, Lisi," he started. It suddenly felt awkward, like he was going to say something really important. But what he said was not at all what I was expecting.

He cleared his throat. "I ran into Brett earlier today. Well, anyways, I guess he and I are kinda cool now, from like, how we hung out last week during the interview and stuff. Who knew, right? So he said he's having a party Saturday. Parents out of town, you get the idea. He told me to stop by."

Pause.

"Anyways, it's not like I'm gonna go there alone. So do you wanna go with me?"

My blood was hammering in my veins. A party at Brett's house? I'd never been inside Brett's house. Come to think of it, I'd never been to a real high school *party*. Not like the kind this would be. The kind that was full of Populars like Brett and Jacqueline.

I was trying to figure out how to sound excited but not *too* excited when Johnny blurted, "Oh, and Bella, too, of course. We could all go."

"Yeah, totally!" I said, regaining my grasp on

normalcy. "Johnny, I can't believe you're hooking us up. Mister popular all of a sudden," I joked, shoving him in the arm.

He pretended to straighten out his wrinkled green As Seen on TV tee. Just then the bell rang.

"Come on, we're late," he said.

I lifted my bag off the floor and swung it over my shoulder. "For a very important date."

Chapter 14

Tuesday, 4p.m.

"You know, I do actually occasionally have home-work," I said, trudging behind Bella. It was about four o'clock in the afternoon but on a Tuesday, the mall was pretty dead.

"Come on, I promise we won't be here too long." Bella yanked open one of the doors to the Meadowhill Mall. "I just know those shoes won't still be there if I don't get them soon, and I need you to see them to make sure I'm not insane."

"See?" Bella said when we were inside Sammy's Shoe Emporium. "With jeans and my cranberry top with the slouchy neck?" She was holding out a satiny magenta pointy-toed slingback. I had to admit it was really cute.

"Very *Sex and the City.*"

"And with my new Levi's? Right? I'm going for 'Come and get me, Mason.'"

While we waited for the salesgirl to return with a box in Bella's size, we wandered around the Shoe Emporium. I had told Bella about Brett's party less than an hour ago, just after the final bell. And now here we were at the mall shopping for outfits for a party we weren't even *technically* invited to. I suppose parties are meant to be a word-of-mouth thing anyway, not like invite-only.

But what was *I* going to wear? More importantly, what was I going to say to Brett? Would it be weird to bring up the other day at the Farmers Market?

Then I saw them. The perfect pair of strappy silver heels. They were like the ones worn by Gwyneth Paltrow at the Academy Awards that winter, a subtle, vintage-looking silver, not all glaring and metallic the way most silver shoes are. The one on display was a size seven. My size.

I slipped my foot right into it and felt like Cinderella. Even in the ratty jeans I was wearing with the ragged hems, the shoe looked elegant.

"*Ooh*," Bella breathed. "So *you*. You must."

"Yes," I said, transfixed by the beauty of my foot. "I must."

About twenty minutes later, we stood with our Sammy's bags in the makeup aisle at CVS, collecting in our red basket as many sweet-smelling ChapSticks as we could find.

"Do you think this is enough?" Bella asked, looking down at our stash.

"The idea is not to inundate but to provide just the right amount to seem like it's still valuable to get." I jiggled the basket full of ChapSticks for emphasis.

"What?"

"It's a supply-and-demand thing. There's a delicate balance. We want to be able to give these out as encouragement, but if we give away too many, then they lose their value. So basically, I'm thinking we need around a hundred ChapSticks." I folded my arms and examined our loot. It was helpful having a father in the advertising business. He'd studied economics in his "youth" and had subjected me and Claire to countless hours of lectures about the patterns of consumerism.

"Then we'll divvy these out to everyone in the club to give away strategically," I continued, "but only for students who actually seem like they might buy a ticket to our booth. And we need breath mints for the boys." I lifted the basket and marched up to the front where the breath mints were sold.

"You're a genius, babe," Bella said. "I knew there was a reason I keep you around. Mo is so going to regret the day she traded us in for Jacqueline."

"Well, lip balm and mints aren't going to beat out a once-in-a-lifetime party in New York City," I said, dumping the contents of the basket onto the checkout counter.

"No," Bella agreed. "But it's a start. Plus . . ." She surveyed the candy at the front counter.

"Plus . . . what?" I was suddenly feeling skeptical again.

"Nothing. I just had a good talk with Trish about the kissing booth is all."

"Why are we involving her again? Isn't she just some random freshman girl? She's not even one of our friends or anything."

"True. But she seems to have a lot of friends."

"So?"

"Who are all interested in buying tickets."

"Why? What did you tell them?"

"Oh, nothing really," Bella said, tossing a bag of Skittles into the pile of supplies we were about to purchase. "I just reminded them that Johnny would be manning the booth. And maybe I hinted that he'd give them more than just a cheek kiss if they help us."

"Bella!"

"What?"

"That's just *wrong*!"

"Lisi, relax, it's no big deal. It's just like you said — we're creating buzz."

"Yeah, but since when is Johnny the main appeal of the booth?"

"Since apparently all the freshman girls think he's like the next Zac Efron or whatever."

"No way." I caught a tube of ChapStick as it rolled to the edge of the counter. "How is that even possible?"

Bella shrugged.

"Well, do you think he knows?" I prodded.

"Doubt it." Bella smirked. "He's kind of oblivious. Actually, I have a little theory. I think maybe he has a secret crush on some girl."

I almost dropped my Sammy's bag. "Are you high? Johnny does NOT have a secret crush. What is it with you and thinking people have secret crushes?"

Bella shrugged. "Why wouldn't he?"

I thought about it. Was it even possible?

No, definitely not.

"Because," I said, "if he did have a secret crush, *we'd* already know about it."

Bella laughed. "Yeah I guess you're right. We pretty much know all there is to know about him."

"Pretty much." That's the great thing about Johnny. He's an open book.

"Anyway, enough about that," Bella said, waving her hand. The elderly cashier lady eyed her with a bemused look. "Can we please get back to the topic of *my* love life, since I seem to be the only person pursuing one these days?"

Ha, I thought as the cashier rang us up. *That's what you think.*

Chapter 15

Wednesday, 8 a.m.

"You were buying outfits for Brett's party? Which is a week away?" Johnny asked, pushing his sunglasses up over his hair, still wet from his morning shower, filling his car with a clean boy smell. I noticed he wasn't wearing his regular glasses. He must have put in contacts, which was weird because he used to complain about how much he hated contacts.

"It's only four days away, it was just shoes, and anyway, that's not the point. The point I'm trying to tell you is that we got kissing booth supplies," I said, indicating several CVS bags I held in my hands before dropping them into the backseat of Johnny's car.

I kind of felt embarrassed just saying the word *kissing* around Johnny, after what Bella had said last night at the mall. I tried to shake the image out of my head, of freshman girls lining up to make out with Johnny. I didn't know why, but I felt possessive of him.

"Incentives?" he asked, starting up the engine as I slid into the front seat and closed the car door with a bang.

"ChapStick and breath mints. Here," I said, handing him a spearmint tin. "On the house."

"Here," he answered. "A ride to school. On the house."

I smirked as I rolled down my window, and we drove in silence for a while.

"Anyway, why do you care if we were shopping for the party?" I asked, watching as the familiar houses passed by the window. I'd grown up on this street, had trick-or-treated in this neighborhood every Halloween, had played hide-and-seek years ago by the big oak tree near the south corner of the park, which was really just a small island of green with a few benches.

The air smelled fresh. Like summer was coming.

"I don't care what you shop for," Johnny said. "I just think you guys are getting really into this party and will probably end up disappointed. I mean, I bet it's going to be pretty lame. In some ways, I'm not sure I even want to go."

"What? Johnny, you have to come!" I could tell he was getting into a mood. They were rare — usually Johnny was the steadiest person I knew — but there were times when he got mysteriously mad at me. It was like boy PMS.

"Why?" he asked. "You and Bella can go do . . . whatever you want to do there. You don't need me. I mean, I guess for the ride, but I'm sure you can get someone else to take you."

"Johnny," I said, loosening my seat belt so I could swivel to face him, my hair blowing all around my head from the open window behind me. I pushed it out of my face. "Stop being cranky. You're coming with us, and that's final. First of all, you're the one who got us invited in the first place. Plus, it'll be way more fun if you're there. Bella is going to throw herself at Mason or someone, and then who will I have to talk to? Anyway, you can bring your Minicam. I'm sure there'll be plenty of fodder for your film there, right?"

And it may be my only chance to see the inside of Brett's home! I thought about Brett's kindness the other day downtown, and it made me feel warm all over. I could still see the pained expression in his eyes as he'd spoken about his father putting pressure on him to succeed — this amazing glimpse into his life that I'd gotten by accident.

And now, in just four days, I'd have the chance for another glimpse.

"Think about it," I added persuasively. "What would Luc Martinez do?"

Johnny brightened at my mention of Martinez — he really worshipped the guy. (Note to self: Pay more attention to Martinez's work; it must actually be pretty amazing. Johnny never has bad taste in film.)

"Yeah, you're right. I can bring my camera." He looked at me and smiled for just a second, then focused again on the road. "Okay, fine, whatever, I'll go to the lame party. And I'll be the chauffeur, as *always*."

"Johnny, you love driving."

He grinned, steering into the front lot. "Got me there."

During lunch that day, we were gathered in the second floor art room, assembling supplies for the booth. I'd never actually taken an art class so I hadn't ever seen the inside of this room except in passing. It had one wall completely covered in supply shelves — paints, pastels, crayons, sketch pads, canvas material, and lots of bottles of chemicals. It had a smell that reminded me of my mom's studio. Above the shelves were drawings by some of the art students. There were big tables with measuring devices built into them. Another thing I noticed was, the blinds were completely pulled back on all the windows, so it was one of the sunniest rooms in the school. I immediately liked it in there.

Dorky Dan had actually *built* a construct that resembled the old kissing booth in the thrift store after I'd described it to him. Now Celeste and Sarah were painting it with burgundy-and-white stripes. They were going for a classic "Parisian awning" look. I really wanted to get my hands on it and cover it in magazine pictures of lips and people kissing, but apparently

Celeste thought that wouldn't be classy enough. I had already made a kissing themed collage, though. Johnny stole it from me and made a paper airplane out of it. Then after tossing it around for a while, he refused to give it back to me, even when I chased him around the art room and knocked over a can of paint.

"Give it back!" I shouted. I was laughing but also kind of serious. I was embarrassed to have my collage thrown around the room where it might get into the wrong hands. Someone might think I was, like, a pervert who liked to stare at pictures of people kissing or something.

"Make me," Johnny said, when I cornered him by an easel. I tried to wrestle it out of his hand and pushed with my other hand against his chest, but he held on tight and I didn't want to rip the collage.

Finally I gave up. "How?" I asked, getting up in his slightly freckled face.

His dark eyes twinkled. "Let me interview you and I'll give it back."

I snorted. "Keep it, then. Hang it on your wall. Enjoy," I said, walking away.

"Will do," he teased.

Bella rolled her eyes at us as she distributed the "incentives" while others tossed some more ideas around. Petra Wu was quizzing herself on something with flash cards. Bella had been worried that Petra's involvement in so many other clubs created a conflict of interest, until Petra reminded her that this meant she could rally that many more people to buy tickets. So I gave her extra ChapSticks.

"Use them wisely," Bella cautioned her, and then we continued making rounds.

Everyone seemed to understand that this year the stakes were different. Jacqueline Winslow had made it a point to compete for first place, and this made us all strangely giddy with anticipation. I could pretty much surmise that no one in our group had ever gone up against one of the Populars for something this big. If at all.

Later that afternoon as I was rushing through the downstairs hall to get my chem book from my locker, I noticed signs littering the walls. KARAOKE IS A-OK! and MR. PETERSON IN THE DUNK TANK! covered the open space near the first cluster of lockers. Farther down, there were signs for bake sales, face painting, and countless other activities. As I approached my locker, I saw some freshmen in the act of hanging a brand-new DANCE DANCE WITH THE FLY GIRLS poster.

But they weren't just any freshmen.

"Trish?" I blurted. Trish stopped what she was doing and handed one of her friends the fat roll of tape she'd been clutching.

"Um. Hi." Trish started fidgeting with the tiny butterfly clip in her hair.

"Hey. We met at the Loews." I eyed her warily.

"Oh, um, yeah."

"So . . . did Jacqueline get you to help with those posters?" I asked, casting my eyes at the partially unrolled Fly Girls banner hanging awkwardly from Trish's friend's hands.

"Oh!" Trish said, coloring. "I. Yeah. Well, the thing is, she was really nice about it. She said I could go to her party if the dance team wins the first prize."

"I thought you wanted to help us with *our* booth?" I didn't mind being blunt. The girl needed to be called out for it.

"Well, that was when we thought your friend Johnny was, um," she blushed more, "available."

"What? First of all, what makes you think Johnny's not available? And I can't believe you'd go back on your word for Jacqueline's pathetic party!" I was surprised at how confrontational I was being with this girl I barely knew. But seriously, I was beginning to think Bella was right, that the Fly Girls really *were* up to some kind of conspiracy against us, and this was just the last straw.

One of Trish's friends whispered something to the other and they laughed.

"What?" I asked, feeling the color come into my own cheeks, but from annoyance, not shyness. Even my ears were hot. "What's so funny?"

"I just said Johnny's cute but he's not as kissable as Zach Braff or anything." The girl shrugged.

"Excuse me, but Johnny Rothberg is very kissable and if you guys don't see it, then you don't deserve a kiss from him anyway." I was *so* annoyed. Who did these little girls think they were, betraying us like that? I turned on the heel of my flip-flop and stomped off. I knew I was acting immature. And, yeah, I was *extremely* embarrassed that I'd just had to defend Johnny to these freshmen girls who knew nothing about him.

But really. Did no one have a conscience anymore?

"They compared Johnny to Zach Braff? Holy hot lips," Bella said into the phone later that afternoon. I sat in the dining room with textbooks stacked around me as late afternoon sun poured in from the big front window.

"Yeah. It's like everyone lately is turning out to be a traitor. I feel like we can't trust anyone anymore." I thought about Mo, how she used to do homework at my house, how we'd help each other with tough assignments. Then we'd order food with my parents. They always loved Mo. She was the reliable one.

What had I done to drive her away?

A slant of sun came through the dining room windows and fell across the big round teak table where I'd spread out my homework. We rarely ate at the dining table anymore, but around that time it was the brightest room in the house.

"Zach Braff, huh?" Bella muttered.

"Bells, I think you're missing the point."

"No, I think I've got it, actually."

"What?" I flipped the pages of my textbook.

"Nothing, I just . . . I was thinking I should make a Facebook group for our kissing booth is all."

"Yeah, Bella, that's a really good idea! Oh, maybe we can make a feature where people can click to send each other a virtual smooch?"

"Girl, you are a genius."

"Hey, that's why they pay me the big bucks."

"You wish."

"Sigh, I know."

"So, hey, did I tell you what Mason said this morning in homeroom?"

"I don't think so."

"He was all 'Do you like Cody Williams?'"

"Oh no."

"No, it's a *good* thing!" Bella explained.

"But Cody Williams is that weird guy who hangs out in the back lot, right? Why would you like Cody?"

"Duh, silly. It means it's working. The plan!"

"Wait. You didn't. Please tell me you did not make out with Cody Williams just to make Mason jealous."

"Well, not exactly. We didn't make out. But I did sit on the hood of his car. And it worked, didn't it? Mason finally noticed!"

I could hear the excitement in Bella's voice. But I couldn't help worrying that her plan had gone too far.

I doodled on the edge of the notebook.

"Well," I sighed at last. "I guess the party Saturday will be the true test. Of his feelings, I mean." Just saying it made my voice catch in my throat. In just a matter of days I'd be hanging out in Brett's house. With Brett. Possibly convincing him to buy a ticket to our kissing booth.

After all, if not Saturday, then when?

Bella was squealing. "You're going to have to come over beforehand to help me get ready for my big night!"

My big night, too, I thought. Brett's party was my chance to turn everything around. Kissing Brett would solve my NBK status. It would confirm all the feelings I'd had bottled up for so long about how right we truly were for each other. Kissing Brett was the answer. And the kissing booth was the only way.

Little did Johnny know when he extended the invite to us that he was finally paving the road for me to have my dream come true.

Chapter 16

Thursday, 11 a.m.

Brian DeLancy pummeled toward me in a muddy T-shirt, his broad shoulders blocking the sun, sweat flying from his freckled brow.

At the last second, I chickened out and stepped away from his path to a chorus of "boo," "aw man!" and "what the hell?" I spun around as Brian sailed past, aimed, and kicked the soccer ball between the two orange end cones.

It was *so* unfair to have girls and boys on the same teams, but that's how gym class worked, and it was either swim with the sharks or drown. Or something like that. We didn't have the kind of gym teachers at Northside who let girls sit out of games if we complained. Complaints meant you had to do laps of the field after class. No, it was far better to just *appear* to be participating, and try to stay out of the line of fire as much as possible.

Which was what I had been doing until Brady, Brian's bigger, scarier cousin who was also in our class, jogged up to my side right after that fateful play. Brady was on my team — teachers always separated Brian and Brady. Divide and conquer — and he was probably going to berate me for once again failing to stop the ball.

But instead, he cleared his throat and appeared to be trying to smile. It looked more like a grimace, but that wasn't really his fault, just the meaty shape of his head. "Yo, Jared," he said. "You part of that kissing booth thing I heard about?"

I nodded warily. I was still waiting for him to say something along the lines of "if you don't find a reason to sit out of the next game, you can kiss my fill-in-the-blank."

"So is it true?" Brady asked.

"Is what true?"

"About Natalie Portman?" He looked really serious.

"I have no idea what you're talking about, Brady. Sorry."

He didn't grace me with any further response, just ran off to join the other jocks. Maybe he'd been hit in the head one too many times.

For the rest of the game, I was sent after all the stray balls — a privilege usually reserved for Freddy

Harcourt, the fattest kid in class. But I really didn't mind. It gave me a chance to slowly jog after them while daydreaming and enjoying the weather.

Then a particularly feisty kick sent the ball out of the field and bouncing off the fence that divided the upper field from the tennis courts. I jogged toward it lazily, taking in the acrid scent of the fresh fertilizer they put down on the fields every spring. It was a nasty smell, but it signaled that the end of the school year was fast approaching, and so it was a happy association. As I ran, my thoughts reverted to Brett's upcoming party. This event vied with the kissing booth for taking up the most space in my brain. In fact, my thoughts about the party were so consuming that I didn't notice anyone else in my line of vision until I was a few feet away and —

Brett had his tennis racket tucked under one tan arm and was standing with his weight on one foot, looking at me with a smirk on his face that made my whole body shiver.

I simultaneously tried to catch the ball as he threw it in my direction while also adjusting my gross old gym tank top and shorts combo, resulting in an awkward fumble.

Brett laughed. "Careful there, Lisi."

He remembered. This time, he remembered. It must have been because of our talk the other day at the Farmers Market. *He knew my name.* I looked at him. He was squinting, just like he had been that Sunday when he had pointed out his dad's business.

"Thanks," I said, trying to quickly think of something more profound to say. But he beat me to it.

"My pleasure," he said.

And then he was gone, and I was running back to the game with a grin on my face so wide and unstoppable that not even the DeLancy boys could scrape it off.

Later that day, I stood staring into my locker, trying to remember which books I needed for my next class. But all I could see were Brett's eyes and his smile. *My pleasure,* he'd said. What did that mean? That he liked helping me out? That he liked *me*? Or was he just being his perfect, polite self?

I felt someone tapping my shoulder, waking me from my reverie. It was rare to be approached at my locker, since it was in the downstairs back hall, which was now almost empty. It was the absolute worst place for a locker. I hoped as I turned around that I wasn't being cornered by a hall monitor. Had I been so caught up in my daydreaming that I hadn't heard the bell?

But then I saw the girl standing behind me, looking nervous. Some girl I had never seen before, in tiny khaki shorts and a white halter top that showed her bra straps. Definitely not a hall monitor.

"I was just wondering . . . is that you?" the girl asked, pointing at a poster down the hall. It said THE SMOOCH-TASTIC SEVEN and listed all of our names.

"Yup, why?" I asked, finally remembering I needed my history book. I turned back, grabbed that and my notebook, and shut the locker.

"So you *are* Lisi Jared. I thought so. I'm Karen. I saw the Facebook page for the kissing booth." Ah. Bella had mentioned making one. But I'd been too busy to go online yet today and check it out.

"Well, I was just wondering if, like . . ." the girl looked starry-eyed.

"Wondering if?" I prodded, now worried I really *would* be late to class.

"Well if it's true. About, you know, Zac."

"Zac who?"

"Efron," Karen answered, blushing and gazing down at her toes.

"I have no idea what you're talking about," I said. Zac Efron? Had he done anything newsworthy lately?

"Oh." The Karen girl seemed disappointed. "Well, like, never mind, then."

I shook my head. People at this school were so weird and celebrity-obsessed. But the girl still stood there in front of me.

"So are you going to be at Brett Jacobson's party Saturday?" she asked.

I was startled. How did this girl know about the party? Jeez, did everyone know? Was the whole school invited?

I nodded slowly. Just then the bell rang, signaling the beginning of sixth period.

"Cool, see ya there!" Karen answered over her shoulder, hurrying off to class.

"Yeah," I muttered, shaking my head again before running off in the opposite direction with my books.

By the time I got to history, I was a full two minutes late. Mr. Welling lifted his fluffy white eyebrows at me and glanced at the clock on the wall as I slinked in and sat in the back. Teachers at Northside always made a big deal out of tardiness. They felt the need to act like it was a personal affront if you missed the first *second* of class, like the part where they were shuffling their papers or writing something illegible on the board.

"Turn to page one-sixteen of the reading," Mr. Welling said. Everyone drearily flipped open their books. "Who can tell me what yellow journalism is?"

The word *journalism* made me immediately think of *Northside Outlook*, and thus of Brett. I wondered if I'd ever know all there was to know about him, his conflicts, his dreams, what he was thinking behind those squinting, sparkling eyes.

Tim Dockson raised his hand in the front row. "It's when the media exaggerates the truth in order to manipulate the masses, basically like brainwashing."

Mr. Welling nodded. "Exaggeration is one way to put it. Some would say the term extends to blatant lying. I want you to examine the passages in the next four pages and highlight all examples of yellow journalism."

I stared at the ginormous history book open on my desk, but all I could think about was Brett's party. We would have to arrive late, but not too late. Was nine too late? Or too early? We definitely couldn't be the first people there. He had a big house, I knew that much. I'd driven by it plenty of times, examining the elaborate Japanese-inspired landscaping on the front lawn.

So we'd enter and people would be having some kind of funny conversation in the living room about music or politics. When I walked into the room, he'd look over at me the way he did on the field earlier. He'd leave his conversation to offer me some snacks. I'd thank him, and he'd say, "My pleasure." Just like he had earlier today. Then we'd share a knowing look, and that would seal the deal. It would be our inside thing.

During the party I would make an effort to mingle a little so as not to look too pathetic. But then I would find Brett again and we would go into the den or the study and he'd show me old copies of *Northside Outlook*. This would be my chance. Somehow, I'd casually mention that I was working on the kissing booth. I'd roll my eyes and make it seem like it was this slightly lame thing that was out of my control, and we'd share that look again. He'd nod sympathetically and then say something about how he'd do his best to make it *less tedious* for me.

Then I would get Johnny to drive me home later on, waving good-bye to Brett across the crowded room as we left. He'd catch my eye and nod. I'd smile. Johnny and Bella would ask me why I was smiling, and I wouldn't answer, I'd just float to the car.

"Why are you smiling?"

"Hmm?" I snapped out of it.

"I just didn't think the USS *Maine* was really that funny," Jason said to me. He was this boy who always wore the same green sweater and seemed slightly over-eager about everything. He also kind of looked like an old man. I noticed he never wore jeans, only pants — one might even call them "slacks." He was one of those premature adults. I could picture him smoking a pipe.

Somehow the image of Jason smoking a pipe in class combined with the way he said "USS *Maine*" made me laugh, in a snorting kind of way.

"Ooookay, guess I just missed the punch line." Jason looked at me funny. I laughed more. Mr. Welling looked over and I put my hand over my mouth, trying to stop laughing. "Seriously, what is so funny?" There is something truly hilarious about a person like Jason asking *what is so funny?* I looked down again at my book, trying to keep from making a scene.

"Okay, well, if you won't tell me what's so funny, maybe you can answer another question for me," Jason tried again.

I sighed, the giggles spent. "Sure. What's up?"

"Is it true?"

"Is what true? Oh, wait, wait a minute. Stop. Are you going to ask me about a celebrity? Did Natalie

Portman and Zac Efron hold hands and leap off a cliff or something?" I demanded.

"I don't know what you're talking about," Jason said. "I'm just wondering if it's true that Mr. Welling is having an affair with the new basketball coach, Ms. Lewis?"

"Oh." I giggled again. "Nope, I'm pretty sure Mr. Lory has dibs on her."

"Well, that makes more sense." Jason finally smiled. "Mr. Lory *is* attractive. In a fatherly sort of way. And I'm not surprised someone has staked a claim on her. Ms. Lewis is a very good-looking woman." Jason had a crush on Ms. Lewis? Would wonders never cease?

Luckily, just then the bell rang.

"Here," I said, handing Jason a tin of breath mints. "For the kissing booth."

Jason looked stunned as I hustled out the door, but as I entered the hallway, a hand immediately stopped me.

It was Mo. For a second, I was flooded with happiness just to see her. But then she grabbed my arm and dragged me against the lockers outside of Mr. Welling's classroom. I noticed she was wearing a really cute yellow jumper over gray tights.

"Is it true?" she demanded.

This was getting REALLY annoying.

"Is WHAT true?" I asked, a little — okay, *a lot* — louder than I normally would. Especially since I hadn't had a single real conversation with Mo now in almost two whole weeks, a fact which I had been obsessing over, trying to figure out what I'd done to make her angry.

It was pretty obnoxious of Mo to avoid me like the plague and then all of a sudden grab me in the hall and accost me. Even if she was trying to end our friendship for no real reason, she could *at least* be a little more polite about it.

No such luck. Mo crossed her arms. "You know what."

"I seriously don't." I crossed my arms, too.

"Matthew McConaughey ring any bells?" Mo's dark brown eyes bore into mine meaningfully.

"Oh. My. GOD!" I threw my arms in the air. "Why is everyone asking me random questions about movie stars?" I asked, not even trying to keep my voice at a moderate level anymore.

"I see how it is," Mo half sneered. Then she turned abruptly and sauntered off.

I leaned back, banging my head against a locker. I was beginning to suspect that *I* saw how it was, too.

At least, I now had a feeling I could guess *who* was behind the weirdness of the day. A certain someone with a flair for exaggeration.

Chapter 17

Friday, 3p.m.

The air was light and breezy, birds were chirping in the low trees in front of the school, and kids flooded from the main doors, laughing and shouting. It was a Friday afternoon full of possibility. Everything was springy and cheerful.

Except for me. I continued pacing by the flagpole. *Where was Bella?* Hiding out from me, no doubt. Well, she'd better emerge soon, because she had some explaining to do.

Like why over the last twenty-four hours I had been approached by at least eleven different people asking me strange questions about movie stars. People had also started looking at me differently in the halls. Petra had given me a thumbs-up from across the cafeteria for no apparent reason.

Johnny was no help — he hadn't talked to Bella

since Wednesday and was in an intense phase of film editing, which meant it was pretty much all he thought about twenty-four-seven. This was how he got — I remembered it from the time he was putting the finishing touches on his family reunion documentary, which won the seventh-grade Art Fest Prodigy Award. No one heard a word from him for days prior. He was kind of like my mother in that way.

I twisted my hair around my finger. I hated being stressed. First, there was the kissing booth. Technically, I was still nowhere near getting Brett to be my first kiss, and I was still completely unprepared for what was to come at Spring Carnival. And the thing was, I actually *cared*. I really wanted to win. Or to beat Jacqueline's booth, at the very least. I couldn't totally explain why. But didn't we deserve to win as much as Jacqueline did? Were people like Jacqueline simply born blessed to date people like Brett and win every competition they entered?

No, it just wasn't fair.

Second, there was Brett. Brett, who was finally noticing my existence. Brett, who, if he didn't kiss me at the kissing booth, might never kiss me, and I'd have to live my whole life knowing I had missed my chance. Brett, whose party was tomorrow night. I didn't know how to act at a party like that. What if I didn't know anyone else there? What if I stood out as the one who didn't belong, and looked like a complete idiot?

Then there was of course the fact that Mo, my best friend up until two weeks ago, had suddenly ditched me and was now not only ignoring me at school — except for when she attacked me in the hall for no reason — but had clearly gone so far as to try to sabotage the kissing booth by helping out the Fly Girls instead.

If that wasn't enough to make my head explode, there was the fact that the entire school seemed to think I had turned into *E!* overnight and I just knew Bella had to be behind whatever gossip was going around. Also, part of me had been really worrying about the fact that Bella had been throwing herself at Mason to no avail and could seriously get hurt if things kept going the way they were. And Johnny, my one sane friend . . . well, Johnny was mostly normal. But that wasn't exactly reassuring right now. I needed to talk to Bella and find out what was going on, ASAP. That was, at least, one thing I could control the outcome of.

"Lisi!"

I turned in the direction of the caller, but instead of Bella, the voice belonged to someone I didn't recognize. *Not again.* I ducked behind a tree. I couldn't handle another awkward encounter — not until I got to the bottom of whatever was going on.

I was beginning to think Bella wasn't going to show. I'd texted her several times after school yesterday — right after the incident in the hall with Mo — but Bella had said she was going out to dinner with her mom. Then I had simply been accosted by so many random people today that I'd had no chance to track her down. Just before lunch, Bella had texted to say she was "wrking on smthing." Finally, I had texted back telling her to meet me at the flagpole at three, adding "hp," which stood for "high priority" and which we only ever used for extreme situations, like the time Bella's grandfather had a heart attack, or the time she sat on a mini blueberry muffin in homeroom and made me change into her gym clothes so she could wear my clothes for her world literature oral. Come to think of it, Bella was usually the one sending the "hp" texts. And I had been there for her every time.

It was 3:20. I shut off my phone and jammed it into my bag. I was about to give up when I heard a familiar laugh. I emerged from behind the tree. Coming out of the side door were Bella, Celeste, and Sarah Singer, who was laughing like crazy with that grating laugh of hers at something Bella had said. Celeste high-fived Bella as they parted ways and Bella headed over to where I stood.

"There you are!" Bella called, smiling widely as she approached, as though she hadn't known *exactly* where I had told her to meet. Or that we weren't supposed to meet twenty minutes ago.

"Did you just high-five Celeste? Who does that?"

"I do!" Bella handed me a Blow Pop.

"No, thanks. We need to talk," I said, adjusting the straps on my pink backpack, suddenly nervous. This had been quite the week of confrontations.

"It's blue raspberry!"

"Bella, seriously. Please. You have to tell me what is going on. Did you say something . . . to anyone . . . about me?"

"About you? No . . . I haven't said anything about you, per se, to anyone, per se. . . ." Bella said, unzipping her bag and getting out her hairbrush. Uh-oh. She always brushed her hair while she strategized.

"Bella. Let me put it this way," I said, placing my hands on my hips to steady myself. "Can you think of a single reason why Brian DeLancy's cousin Brady would ask me a question about Natalie Portman? Or why Mo practically threw me against the lockers yesterday after U.S. history? Or why a significant portion of the NHS population has been shouting celebrity names at me like I'm a red-carpet paparazzo?"

"Paparazzo?"

"That's the singular of *paparazzi*. Bella, I know that you know that I know that you are behind this, so just tell me. Tell me what you said. Whatever it is, I'm sure it's just a misunderstanding. But I am going to seriously lose my mind if I don't get to the bottom of this. I need some answers. Now."

Wow. I sounded kind of like my dad when he got mad at Claire for staying out all night during Senior Week last year. She hadn't called and then had lied, saying she'd slept over at her best friend Jen's house — when in reality she had slept over at Gary Emerson's. But nothing had *happened* because a bunch of other people were there, too, and Gary had fallen asleep by the pool while the rest of the kids had just watched bootleg DVDs on his parents' television, and Claire had had to sleep on the hard floor that was covered in gummy bears for some reason. A couple days later she'd told me the whole story but had made me swear never to tell Mom and Dad — which was why our dad had been so angry when Claire had come home the next morning, her hair sticking out every which way and gummy bears stuck to her clothes.

But Bella wouldn't lie to me. She couldn't. Though she *was* looking at me kind of funny, through the tent of perfectly smooth hair that cascaded across her face as she brushed it.

"See."

"See what?" I asked, looking around at the smattering of short trees on the front lawn surrounding the flagpole.

"This is why I didn't want to tell you." Bella sighed and flipped her hair back over her shoulder, focusing her doe-brown eyes on mine. "I knew you'd react this way."

"What way?"

"Uptight."

I grabbed the hairbrush out of Bella's hand. "Maybe I wouldn't be so uptight if my best friend wasn't keeping secrets from me!"

"First of all, *I'm* not keeping any secrets," Bella retorted, yanking the brush back and putting it safely away in her bag. "*I* seem to be the only one who's *not* keeping secrets. I simply did what I had to do to pique everyone's interest in the kissing booth. You said yourself that ChapStick and mints weren't going to be enough to convince people, that we'd need a better marketing campaign, as you put it. I was simply upholding my end of the bargain."

"So what *exactly* did you say?"

"Come on, walk with me," Bella said, turning from me and heading toward Washington Avenue which leads to the part of town we live in. "So here's the thing. You gave me the perfect idea the other day, when we were talking about how the freshman girls lost interest in kissing Johnny. I realized we had to, you know, up the ante!"

"I'm not following," I said, though I was in fact following Bella as we cut across the school lawn. "What does this have to do with Natalie Portman?"

"Actually, I have no idea who started the Natalie Portman rumor. But I suppose any publicity is good publicity!"

"So? What did you do?"

"Well, I may have put a post on the new Facebook page for the kissing booth. You know how you suggested making a group? Great idea, by the way!"

"You've been updating the Facebook page?" I asked, feeling behind.

"Yeah! I've been waiting since yesterday for you to notice, but I guess *some* people are too caught up in themselves right now." Now *Bella* thought I was too caught up in myself? Would wonders never cease? "Hey, even Johnny joined the group already. Celeste, Sarah, Petra, Dan. We're all on there. In fact, we already had forty-five members last time I logged on," Bella said proudly. She was walking just far enough in front of me that I couldn't see her expression.

"Go on," I insisted. "What did you say on the Facebook page?" I was starting to have a really bad feeling about where this was going.

Bella paused as though choosing her words carefully. "I simply suggested that there'd be a special guest at the kissing booth. Someone that a lot of people would be interested in. Like a celebrity appearance sort of thing. A secret guest."

"A *celebrity* appearance?" It was all starting to fall into place. Though I still didn't understand why everyone assumed I knew anything about it. I was walking faster now to keep up with Bella. "Why would you say that? We don't know any celebrities."

"*I* don't know any celebrities," Bella agreed. "But *you* do! Or at least, your dad does, right? Which is what I explained to Celeste. I mean Cliff's always mentioning all the people he's done ads with." Bella always refers to other people's parents by their first names. "I'm sure he can get us someone great. It'll be easy! And you'll have me to thank when the kissing booth sells the most tickets."

And I would have been appalled by where the

conversation had gone if it hadn't sounded quite so ridiculous. But really. Bella had to be joking.

"Ha-ha. Right. So what did you *really* tell everyone?"

"All I said was that your dad has connections and could get us a surprise guest for the booth," Bella said, perfectly serious. "I'm surprised so many people bothered you, since I said it was top secret and that you didn't like to talk about your family network. It's not my fault if Celeste blabbed about Cliff's connections." Bella shrugged again as if this were the most normal thing in the world.

"Wait. Seriously?" It was just absurd enough that it might actually be true. "Bells, Cliff — uh, my dad — is *not* friends with celebrities. You know that, right? Just because he was on the set of that *one* Rachel Bilson Crest commercial two years ago does not mean that he's best buds with her — or anyone else famous, for that matter."

"But he works for, like, the biggest ad agency in Chicago. They all have connections to all the hot actors, don't they? I can't see why, if he explained it's for our Spring Carnival and all, that he couldn't get us Zac Efron or an equivalent. What's the big deal? I mean, once Zac realizes what a great photo op this would be, donating time to a local high school . . . with a charity at stake, too . . . I mean, it's not like I didn't think this through."

"Um, Bella, you *didn't* think this through. Did it not even occur to you to ask me? Does my opinion on the matter even *count*? It is going to be seriously impossible to make this happen, and now the entire school is going to think we're frauds. Liars. I'm just — I'm just so —"

"Uptight?"

"Excuse me?" Now I *really* couldn't really believe my ears. Was Bella actually trying to pick a fight with me?

"No offense or anything." Bella stared ahead at the sidewalk. "It's just that you can't ever loosen up, Lisi. You're so tense. Ever since we decided to do this kissing booth, I knew you'd find a way to bail out on everyone."

"I didn't realize at the time that we'd basically be waging war with the most popular girls in the school!" I said, feeling my voice reaching a pitch best saved for birds and dolphins.

"Exactly! None of us did! That's *exactly* why I needed to step up our game — why I needed to act in the moment. Trust me, Lisi," Bella said, putting her hand on my upper arm.

I sighed and stopped walking. Bella stopped, too.

"Maybe I should put up a new post," I offered, "saying we won't be able to invite the special guest after all."

Bella pouted. "And just give up?"

"Isn't it worse if we lie about having a guest who then never materializes?"

Bella chewed her lip. "Maybe one *will* materialize? If we play our cards right? Can't you at least ask your dad?"

"Bella . . ." I started.

"Even if it doesn't happen, for reasons beyond our control, we certainly can't be blamed, after the fact . . . once the tickets are sold, if you see what I mean."

"So you're saying as long as we keep up the lie, we'll sell tickets."

"Well, when you put it that way, it sounds all deceitful!"

I shook my head, at a loss for words. She was right in a way. The damage had already been done. Correcting it would mean folding early and bowing out.

"We'll figure out a way to make this work. Okay?" Bella said. "Come on, we're on the same side here, right?"

I shifted my weight. "I mean, yeah. We're on the same side." I finally gave in. "I just, I wish you wouldn't have gone behind my back." We started walking again.

Bella smiled as we turned the corner and approached the broad front stoop of her house. "Just check out the Facebook page. It's really pretty cool-looking. And besides," she paused, flicking hair out of her face, "I'll make it up to you. Come over before the party tomorrow and I'll make you beautiful. That is, *more* beautiful."

I felt my cheeks flush at the mention of Brett's party again. Was I really ready? Well, if anyone could help me prepare, it was Bella. I sighed again.

"Deal," I finally said.

Bella squealed, she hugged me quickly, and then dashed up her front stairs, leaving me to walk the rest of the way down the street toward my own house.

I just needed to think.

I'd gotten the talk with Bella over with. But now I had an even bigger problem to solve: How was I ever going to get us a celebrity guest?

Chapter 18

Friday, 4p.m.

When I pushed the front door open, I could hear the phone ringing in the kitchen.

"Hey, honey! Can you grab that?" my mom's voice asked, drifting through the closed study door.

I threw my backpack on the stairs and sauntered into the kitchen, grabbing the cordless off the counter and opening the refrigerator door at the same time.

"Hello?"

"Lis?"

"Johnny? Why are you calling my house phone?" I leaned into the fridge and stared at the old milk, diet soda, and mustard. Yup, mom was in the zone preparing for her big show — as she had been all week — and her work had taken its toll on the status of our groceries.

"Dude, your phone's off. Did you forget to charge it or something?"

"I shut it off earlier. My bad," I said, dragging a bag of limp-looking carrots out of the vegetable bin. "So what's up?"

"Nada. Just sent out some clips of my work."

"Nice," I said. Every few months, Johnny sends out new demo material to various film agencies in LA and New York and lots of indie organizations, trying to get noticed. So far he hadn't really heard back from anyone, but still. It was far more impressive than anything I'd ever done.

"So now, you know, it's just the Friday night blues." Johnny sighed.

I could tell by his voice that he was probably lying on his bed. Johnny had this whole pessimistic outlook regarding weekends — he said the way normal people get depressed on Sunday nights, knowing another week of school was beginning, he would get depressed on Friday nights, knowing that the weekend was just beginning but was going to be over so soon.

"Me, too. I feel like I've barely seen you all week."

"Miss me?"

"Actually, you are officially the most sane person in my life." I threw the bag of carrots into the garbage under the sink and pulled open the drawer where we keep take-out menus. I sank into one of the kitchen chairs and started fiddling with a pen that was lying there.

"Not sure if that's a compliment, but I guess I'll take it. So how's the ChapStick bribery going?"

It was my turn to give an exaggerated sigh. "So you haven't heard yet? Well, at least I wasn't the *last* loser in our school to find out. You'll never believe this. I found out where all those rumors came from. I'll give you a hint, it starts with a B."

"Bethlehem? Botswana? Banana Republic? What rumors?"

"I'll give you another hint," I said, doodling on the edge of an Italian menu. "It ends in *ella*."

"What'd she say? I haven't heard anything."

"Oh you know, nothing *unreasonable*," I said in Bella's melodramatic tone. Johnny laughed. "She just told *a few* people on Facebook that I would somehow secure a 'special celebrity guest' to appear at the kissing booth."

I had doodled a smiley face on the menu, and now drew a bunch of arrows running through it at different angles.

"Who's the guest?" There was a clicking sound in the background.

I put down my menu. I rocked back in my chair. "Are you going through your DVD collection again while I'm trying to talk to you?" I could recognize that clicking sound anywhere.

"Um, are *you* staring at a food menu while *I'm* trying to talk to *you*?" Johnny asked.

I smiled, guilty. "Nope."

"Liar. Lemme guess, Thai?"

"Johnny, don't you want to hear the rest of my story? So Bella said I would get a celebrity. She didn't say who. She just said my dad could hook us up with someone big. Can you believe that? I mean, has she lost it completely? She told everyone in school this big lie and now what am I supposed to do?"

I knew I was ruining the back legs of my chair by leaning back so far, but I didn't care.

"Well, can he? Your dad?"

"No! I mean, well, at least, I assume not."

"Hm. Have you asked him yet?"

"Wait a sec, whose side are you on anyway?" I asked.

"Jeez, can't a guy inquire into the details? Anyway, I wouldn't worry about it. It's just one of many Bella schemes. It'll work itself out. Always does. Holla holla holla! Found it!"

"Johnny, I *knew* it. I knew you were going through your precious film library."

"I found the Kubricks!" Johnny had a lot of illegally burned DVDs. He always justified it by claiming that what he contributed to the film world far outweighed what he stole from it. But he wasn't always great about labeling them, so it sometimes took a million tries to find the right one.

"Congrats."

"Oh, come on. *Clockwork Orange? The Shining?* Show a little enthusiasm for the classics! Wanna come over and have a marathon? My mom's making pierogi. Cheesy potatoey goodness followed by twisted psychological thrillers — what more could a girl want?"

I smiled. Then frowned. "Ugh, no, I should probably order food for me and my mom. God knows she won't get around to feeding herself otherwise, and believe me, the results of that would be worse than a psychological thriller."

I stared at the menu in front of me. The words seemed to blur together.

"Hey," Johnny said. I could picture him draped dramatically across his hideous plaid duvet. "I know what would convince you to come over."

"What?"

"If I showed you my interview with Brett and Mason. Not that I'm going to."

"Johnny," I said. I *did* want to watch that footage. But how did he know? Did he suspect we'd stolen the other DVD? I suddenly felt too exhausted to keep talking, let alone try to figure out what he was getting at. "I'm just . . . so stressed out. I don't think I even have it in me to leave the house right now."

For some reason, as I was talking, I felt my throat closing up. Almost like I was going to cry. It had been such a long week. I leaned over the table, cradling my head in my arm.

"You okay? I mean about this whole celebrity whatever thing?" Johnny sounded a little concerned. Which was nice of him and everything. But it didn't really help.

Everything was too confusing, with Mo and Brett and Bella. Everything felt like it was falling apart.

I felt like my life up until spring break had been a photograph of me and my friends together. Now it was a collage of us, all cut up into separate segments. No, not even a collage. We were just the pieces, still unglued. And it felt like there was a breeze coming, about to blow us all in opposite directions forever.

I felt like there was so much I'd never know how to solve, let alone what to order for dinner.

I tried to take a deep breath, but my throat still felt kind of ragged. "It's fine. I mean, I'll figure it all out. It's just a silly Bella scheme, like you said."

But it wasn't fair. Why did it always seem like I was the one stuck solving problems that other people created? Picking up the pieces, rearranging, gluing it all down?

Then again, the kissing booth had been my own doing. So in a way, it was all my own fault. I'd opened the floodgates. And as far as I could tell, there was no way out of it.

Not with everyone counting on me more than ever.

"Well," Johnny said, clearing his throat. "I'll see you at Brett's tomorrow anyway, right?"

Brett's party. The one thing that hadn't turned into a disaster waiting to happen. At least, not *yet*.

"Yup." I said.

I clicked the phone off and dropped my head onto the table.

I sat like that for what seemed like a really long time. It had almost become a full-blown nap when my mother came up and patted me on the back.

Mom stood near me quietly for a minute. Finally, I looked up. She was staring into space, thinking about something. I rubbed my neck.

"What?" I said.

"Hm?" my mom murmured hazily. "I was just thinking about the ordering. Of the pieces. You know, for my show. I'm still having trouble picturing it."

"It'll come to you, Mom. Just don't force it." It was so much easier giving someone else advice than dealing with my own issues.

My mom smiled. "You're right. Hey, what did you do to this menu?" She picked up the Italian menu covered in fresh doodles and made a clucking sound. Then she picked up the phone, ordered a couple of fettuccines and replaced the phone on the charger.

"Do you know when Dad's getting home tonight?" I asked.

"He's traveling, sweetie. He'll be back Monday. Do you need his help with something?"

Help. Yeah. I wanted to ask her why it never occurred to her or Dad to *tell* me before they decided to go all MIA on me.

But I just shrugged. Did I need Dad to help me with something? No. I needed him to make a miracle happen.

*   *   *

Later that night, I finally went online and checked my e-mails. I didn't usually let them get backed up by more than one day, but I'd been so busy and overwhelmed. Or perhaps I was just avoiding reality. Maybe both.

I saw an invitation to join the Spring Carnival's kissing booth group on Facebook and signed on. The page was actually really cute. The group was open only to members of the NHS network. Bella had posted some pictures of us working on making the booth. She'd also added all these cute icons. I saw the "latest news" posting about the special guest and cringed. It DID sound exciting — if I weren't the one expected to some-how make it happen.

And then I looked at my new notifications and saw something startling.

YOU HAVE RECEIVED ONE
ANONYMOUS "SMOOCH" FROM A
MEMBER OF "SPRING CARNIVAL'S
KISSING BOOTH." CLICK HERE TO
SEE ALL MEMBERS OF THIS GROUP.

Me? I had received an anonymous smooch? Was it just from Bella, trying to cheer me up? But, then, why would she have sent it to me anonymously?

I quickly scanned the list of group members. There were now seventy-three. I felt a surge of pride, realizing that many people from our school had taken notice of it. God, where had I *been* the last couple of days?

Oh, yeah, daydreaming about Brett.

Brett Jacobson.

I scrolled through the group.

And there he was.

!!!!!!

Could the anonymous smooch have been from *Brett*?

True, there were seventy-two other people it could have come from.

But who would send *me* an anonymous smooch? It hadn't occurred to me that there might be someone out there who actually wanted to kiss me. Like, me in particular.

I clicked around online for a few hours, until it got pretty late. I knew I wouldn't really be able to sleep, with all this stress haunting me.

Finally, around one in the morning, I crawled into bed and hugged my enormous Pooh Bear pillow. I stared at the collage on my wall near my bed. Despite all the things going on in my life there was only one thing on my mind right now.

I smiled into Pooh Bear's red shirt.

Someone wanted to kiss me.

Chapter 19

Saturday, 9p.m.

My silver sandals glimmered in the moonlight as my long tan legs emerged from the back door of Johnny's car. I felt like a princess.

The night air felt soft and warm and it smelled like the lilacs lining the iron gate that divided the Jacobsons' yard from their neighbors'. Already Brett's driveway was packed with cars, as was the road directly in front of his massive, light gray house. In the twinkle of the faux Victorian streetlamps, the house itself seemed to match the color of Brett's eyes. Japanese-style shrubs lined the front of the house in a serene line, like attendants waiting to greet us as we approached.

I could feel the heels of my shoes sinking into the damp grass. It was one of those nights when the wind is so still that you feel you can hear everything for miles — the humming of the streetlights, the sounds of cars driving through town, and of course the shouting and laughing and the thumping bass from behind the walls of the Jacobsons' home.

For once, both Bella and Johnny were silent at my side. I figured they were both as excited and nervous as I was to be entering the first big blowout party of our high school careers.

I told myself to act normal. But how could I, when I felt like Cinderella arriving at a ball?

I'd worn a pale blue wraparound dress with a white camisole underneath, and the strappy silver Gwyneth Paltrow heels I'd found at Sammy's the other day. Then I had gone to Bella's, where Bella had curled my still slightly too short hair using a straightening iron instead of a curling iron, creating big, luscious waves around my face. She said it looked very Tina Fey.

In addition to my normal thin line of eyeliner, Bella had added a soft lavender shadow to my eyelids, which made my blue eyes even brighter. Then she finished my look with peach-tinted lip gloss. The effect of my whole ensemble was natural, even sweet, but surprisingly sexy, too — mostly because the dress was kind of short and it was too warm out now for tights.

Despite the warmth, I felt goose bumps all over my arms and legs.

Had I overdone it? I didn't want to seem like I was some desperate chick who thought I needed to dress up like it was the prom just for a regular party. I threw a panicky glance at Bella as we approached the three stairs in front of Brett's door.

Bella had worn fitted dark jeans with her new shoes and a flirty silk magenta top from Urban Outfitters. Her outfit looked way more effortless, I thought. Though, of course, I knew that in fact Bella had tried on three red shirts, a maroon tank top, and a frilly white peasant blouse before settling on the one she was wearing now.

Johnny, too, was looking a lot more dapper than usual. Not that I minded his usual snarky T-shirt and baggy pants ensembles, but it was kind of shocking — almost disorienting — to see him in what looked like a *freshly washed* hunter green T-shirt with an actual *collar* — I didn't think I'd seen him in anything with a collar since Michael Gold's bar mitzvah — and his wavy hair was extra dark tonight because it was still wet from a shower. He had his DVD camera attached to one hand as always.

"Do you think I'm overdressed?" I asked anxiously.

Bella rolled her eyes. I'd already asked her this seven times.

"You look good," Johnny answered. "You should wear dresses more. Anyway, you wanna ring it or are we waiting for the party to come to us?" Johnny asked, gesturing to the doorbell. Bella hit the buzzer.

We waited. Nothing happened. The shouting and music continued behind the door.

I shuffled my feet, hearing my new shoes click on the cement stoop. I felt a little like I was going to throw up and considered sitting down on one of the steps. But I didn't want to ruin my dress. Especially since it was actually Claire's.

"Maybe we should just . . ." I trailed off as Bella hit the buzzer again.

Just then the door swung up, bathing us in red light from what must have been the living room off to the right. I squinted as this guy Troy, who I recognized as a trumpet player from the Northside Players, let us pass and shut the door again.

And then we were inside Brett Jacobson's home.

I stumbled into the crowd. There were *tons* of kids here. All the lamps had red lightbulbs in them, casting a glow through the room. At the back of the living room, a big stereo system was set up with an iPhone plugged into it, and what looked like elegant antique furniture — probably part of Mr. Jacobson's expensive collection — was covered hastily in old bedsheets, for easy cleanup apparently. On the mantel, Brett's tennis trophies twinkled in the red light.

Several girls waved to me as I made my way deeper into the cavernous room. The music and voices bounced off the high ceilings, increasing the feeling of chaos and excitement. Lots of people smiled at me like we were good friends. Greg Thompson emerged out of nowhere and kissed me on the cheek!

I kind of couldn't believe how *welcome* I was feeling at the same time that I also felt completely over my head. It was amazing what one slight-exaggeration-slash-bold-faced-lie could do to one's popularity status.

I realized Bella was shouting something at me, but I could barely hear what she was saying.

"Did you hear me?" Bella said again, backing up so her mouth was closer to my ear. "I was just saying . . . stick to The Plan." I nodded and gave her a thumbs-up, then instantly felt stupid and didn't know what to do with my thumb.

The "Plan" Bella was referring to was what we had been discussing at her house earlier that night. I had called my dad and casually mentioned the "celebrity guest" idea — and was met with a big belly laugh.

"Unless you were hoping for the new face of Swiffer's disposable mops," Dad had chuckled.

I begged him to be serious, but he said *I* should be serious. My dad can be kind of intimidating, actually. He told me the kind of clients he worked with paid a high price for celebrity talent. I felt like such a baby, not knowing that already. So I had dropped the subject.

But when I told Bella the bad news — that there was no way Cliff Jared could even put us in touch with the right kind of person for Spring Carnival — Bella had not been fazed. Her response was, "Just keep playing along with it. As long as people *believe* we're going to have a celeb appearance, that's all that really matters, right? We just want them to buy tickets."

"But that's basically lying to the customer," I had countered, feeling increasingly freaked out about the situation.

"We already lied. There's no going back now," Bella had warned. It had hardly seemed fair to point out that Bella was the only one — so far — who'd actually lied about anything. At least explicitly. But she was right, in a way. There was nothing I could say that wouldn't make *all* of us seem like frauds.

For now, anyway, my only real choice was to play along.

And it was working, apparently. At least, if countless smiles and waves from people who had, until now, never acknowledged my existence were any indication.

I scanned the crowd as we made our way through it. Katrina Terrence was dancing in a circle with Cindy Ramirez and a few other Fly Girls right next to a towering bookcase covered in mostly empty plastic cups. Katrina was wiggling her butt around and Cindy was doing some kind of choreographed thing with another girl involving twirling at the same time. They looked like they were having the time of their lives, and for a second, in the crowded sweaty room, even though they hadn't noticed me there, I felt like I was part of it. Part of the scene.

Like it made sense for me to be there.

But just as suddenly, I felt a cold splash down my leg

and realized someone had dropped a cup on my foot. When I looked around, I realized I'd lost Bella and Johnny somewhere in the crowd. Bella had probably gone off to look for Mason. But Johnny — where was he?

I texted Bella.

WHERE R U?

I waited a good thirty seconds, but there was no reply.

I was worried I'd gotten a stain on Claire's dress.

"Hey, Judson," I called to Judson Green, who was grabbing celery sticks from a porcelain bowl and sticking them in his nose. "Do you know where the kitchen is?"

"Yeah, this party's bitchin'!" he yelled and tossed back the rest of his beer, dislodging one of the celery sticks in the process.

"No, *kitchen*, KITCHEN!" I said, shouting in his ear.

"You're lookin' hot tonight, Kitchen Girl," Judson laughed, and I blushed.

"Never mind!" I said, seeing a non-red light down at the other end of the long hallway, with people gathered in a doorway.

I texted Bella again and waited a few seconds. No response.

I entered the kitchen just as several girls wandered out, giggling and carrying sloshing drinks. I flattened myself against the wall as they passed, not really wanting a repeat of the first spill.

And that's when I saw him. Brett was leaning back against a wooden butcher block in the middle of the kitchen, wearing a yellow-and-gray striped shirt. He was talking to a tall blond guy who sported a grungy T-shirt that said NO NONSENSE. I didn't recognize him. Maybe he didn't go to our school?

The kitchen was only lit by the stove light, which meant the room was fairly dim. Behind Brett, the sliding door leading to what looked like a massive backyard was open. Through the screen, I could see a pool with tikki torches around it and more people milling about. There must have been eighty or a hundred kids at Brett's party. I thought I could see a tiny red light, like a laser beam, dodging in and out of the crowd of kids outside. I guessed it was Johnny's camera. *He must be happy that he came,* I thought. This was about thirty percent of our entire school, right here!

Something about that little red dot of light comforted me.

As I edged my way slowly into the kitchen, I noticed a big rectangular glass tank on the large counter to my left, between where I stood and where Brett stood. I was startled for a second to see movement in it, and realized it was a gerbil cage. The creature was darting in and out of a little gerbil hut in the corner of the tank.

I glanced around the enormous kitchen again, wondering if there was any place *I* could hide, but my

eyes kept straying back to Brett. I had completely forgotten why I'd even come to the kitchen in the first place.
It was like my brain went dead when he was around.

As though he could sense me staring, Brett stopped
talking to No Nonsense Guy and turned to look directly
at me. I felt myself blush to my ears.

"You made it." He smiled.

For a second I got confused and glanced over my
shoulder to see if he was talking to someone else. But
the doorway was now empty. He was definitely talking
to me.

"Um, yeah." I smiled a little, then shut my mouth
quickly, not wanting to look like an idiot.

I glanced down at the cage on the counter, desper-
ately trying to think of something interesting to say. "So
what's his name?" is what came out.

"Oh, that's Alex," Brett answered. His light brown
hair looked so soft in the dim light, one section hanging loosely in front of his eye. I wanted to brush it with
my fingers.

Instead I leaned closer to the cage and put my finger
out. The gerbil stuck its nose against the glass. "Hey
there, Alex!" I said. It was much easier talking to rodents
than talking to Brett directly.

But for some reason, Brett and No Nonsense Guy
started cracking up uncontrollably.

I straightened and looked from one to other, feeling
mortified. I glanced down at my dress to see if they

were laughing at the stain (oh, yeah — *that's* why I'd come to the kitchen!).

"What's so funny?" I finally asked, as the guys continued laughing.

"It's just," Brett said, laughing some more. It was hard not to laugh along with him, even though I didn't get the joke. "It's just, *this* is Alex," he said, pointing at No Nonsense. "My cousin."

"Oh!" My face felt so hot, I was worried Bella's careful makeup job was melting off.

"We never actually named that guy," Brett went on, gesturing back at the gerbil.

"You never named your pet?" I asked, forgetting for a moment that I was talking to my crush of three years. *Who didn't name their pets?*

Brett shrugged. "It's my mom's. I think she has a nickname for it or something. I don't know. I pretty much just ignore it."

"Poor gerbil," I muttered.

Brett didn't seem to hear me. Instead he leaned closer. "Did you need, like, a drink or something? Or, uh, what was it, pistachio? Sorry we don't have any nutty ice cream to offer."

He said it so casually, like it wasn't the biggest, most earthshaking moment of my life, that he had remembered my favorite ice cream.

"Ha-ha," I laughed, trying really hard not to snort awkwardly. At least this was going slightly better than the Farmers Market incident.

Brett looked at me for a second, and in that moment, No Nonsense — or Alex, apparently — said to Brett, "I'll catch you later, man. Gotta go shove some ladies into the pool," and then sauntered out the back door.

Suddenly, the kitchen felt very, *very* empty. Why was no one passing through anymore?

Brett laughed a short "heh" kind of laugh. "That guy. He can get away with anything."

"You mean your cousin?" I could hardly believe I was having a *one-on-one* conversation with Brett. Again!

Brett leaned his hip against the counter. He was only, like, a foot and a half from where I was standing. "He can seriously do whatever he wants. It's insane."

"Do you think he's really going to push people into the pool? Should we maybe . . . warn them?" I offered.

But Brett seemed lost in a thought, his eyes focused straight ahead. "No one puts any pressure on him to do things the right way. He dropped out of school once and his parents, my aunt Ginny and uncle Ted, didn't even *say* anything. Uncle Ted actually gave Alex some cash to try starting a business. Then when that went absolutely nowhere, no one was even mad or anything. He just signed up for high school again as though none of it had happened."

"What business was he going to start?"

"That's the whole point! None of us even knows! It's just so ridiculous. Ridiculously unfair. Some of us have to really pull our weight, while others get to do whatever they want and just, like, *enjoy* life."

I heard some girly screams coming through the screen door, followed by loud splashes. We both swiveled toward the noise. Then we heard a bunch of other voices laughing.

It definitely sounded like Alex was enjoying life.

Brett sighed. He turned so he was facing me straight on. We were both quiet for a second, and the moment felt heavy — like something serious was passing between us. After all, he'd told me about his aunt Ginny and uncle Ted.

My pulse quickened and my mind started racing at a manic pace. Oh God. Was this it? Was this the moment? Was Brett the one who had sent me the anonymous Facebook smooch? Should I say something? What was he thinking? Did he sense that I liked him?

All the questions blurred into white noise in my head, which got louder and louder. It was like alarm bells were going off all around me — inside me — and I half expected firemen to appear out of nowhere, sliding down poles.

And then it all came to a screeching halt when he said, "Well, next year none of this will matter. I'll already be at Brown."

"Oh, right," I said. Because Brett was graduating. In a mere month. And then he'd be gone.

And none of this would matter.

I wouldn't matter.

So the kissing booth really was my only chance. That was it. There *were* no other chances. There was no more time to hope and dream. It was kissing booth or never.

I needed to say something. A girl, dripping wet in her jeans and tank top, ran through the back door, looked at us for a second, and then marched past into the hallway and disappeared.

We were alone again.

I adjusted my weight from one leg to the other. "So," I began. "Are you going to the Spring Carnival next Friday?"

Brett stared at me for a second, almost like he didn't know what I meant.

"You know, Spring Carnival?"

He smiled again. And oh, his smile was distracting. "Yeah. I'll be there. Why?"

Why? I hadn't thought that far.

"Oh, nothing. I'm just, my friends and I. We have a booth. I think, I mean maybe you've seen our Facebook page. It's just this like — "

"The kissing booth? I know."

I nodded.

He breathed in and out slowly. "So you'll be working at the kissing booth? At the fair?"

By now I could feel my ears burning again. "Well, sort of. I mean, yeah." I tried to shrug, like it wasn't a big deal — like it wasn't the *biggest deal ever.*

I looked at Brett. His eyebrows were drawn together like he was concentrating or solving a math problem. But all he said was, "Cool."

Meanwhile, my heart was beating a mile a minute. I swallowed. I took a deep breath. I glanced ever so fleetingly at my phone screen. Still no texts. I looked up again. And then, slowly, subtly, I inched a bit closer to Brett.

"So," I said quietly, hoping my voice wasn't wavering as much as it seemed like it was. "Congratulations, I guess. On getting into Brown or whatever."

He leaned in toward me, his blue-gray eyes particularly dark. "Yeah, thanks. I guess." He had a tiny half-smile on his lips. And yet his eyes looked sad.

Do something! I told myself. But what? Just lean in and kiss him on the lips? Those lips that were smiling slightly at me right now? He'd think I was a freak.

My heart felt like it was spinning around and around on the gerbil's wheel. Brett edged even closer.

"Hey," he whispered.

I was starting to feel dizzy. His face was getting closer.

He was parting his lips!

And then, just as he was so close to me I could feel his breath, he spoke.

And what he said was:

"Jacqueline."

Chapter 20

Saturday, later

I almost choked. *Jacqueline*? "I'm Lisi!" I blurted out, and I heard a gasp from behind me and swiveled around.

There in the entrance to the hallway stood Jacqueline, along with the girl formerly known as my best friend, Mo. Jacqueline wore a little white skirt and even tinier polo shirt. Mo was wearing a miniskirt over blue leggings and a black tank top. They looked pretty, I thought. And pissed.

Jacqueline squinted at me. "Who is *this*?" she sneered.

"I, I'm —" I started to say, but she cut me off.

"If you have something you wanna tell Brett, maybe you can tell all of us, huh?" Jacqueline said, approaching me. I instinctively raised my hands to protect myself.

What was she going to do? She seemed really angry. She had this animal look in her eyes.

I held my breath as she lunged for me, grabbed the edge of my dress and yanked me away from Brett, who had already taken a step back.

"Well, Lisi? What do you have to tell Brett that's so important? Enlighten us," she goaded.

Hah. Well, there you go — she *did* know who I was. But that didn't exactly help my situation at the moment.

"Um, I was just, we were talking about, um —"

"Let me guess. The infamous kissing booth I've heard so much about. Could you be more juvenile?" She was right up in my face now, and I noticed her skin wasn't really as clear as it seemed from afar. But she was still insanely beautiful. And, right now, horrifying. Kind of like a panther about to pounce. I was already backed up against the counter, and Mo was standing in the doorway. I had nowhere to escape.

"Grow up," Jacqueline spat. "Do you really think anyone in this school is going to *pay actual money* to make out with *you?*" Jacqueline started laughing, as if this were the most hilarious thing she'd ever said.

I stood there, at a loss for words. No one had ever been so, well, *mean* to me in my entire life. I couldn't tell if I was more angry or more shocked.

Brett started to interrupt her laughter. "Jacks," he said. "This isn't necessary."

"Yeah, you know what's not necessary? Girls like her," she said, giving me a shove in the shoulder that actually really hurt.

Then she grabbed hold of Brett's arm and whispered not too quietly through clenched teeth, "We have to talk. *Now.*"

I was still frozen there in shock as Jacqueline dragged Brett out the screen door and into the dark night.

But apparently my torture wasn't over yet.

"So. What were you doing?" Mo had folded her arms and was leaning back against the doorframe glaring at me skeptically. I still hadn't quite gotten used to the Mo-fro and stared at it as if searching for an answer to Mo's question.

My mouth had gone dry and I almost wanted to say "Bubble dubsters," to see if she had any gum, but thought better of it. Besides, I was worried I might start crying. Instead I took a deep breath and tried to calm myself.

"Feeding the gerbil," I finally responded, gesturing at the tank. I knew it didn't make any sense. But then, neither did Mo's coldness toward me.

Mo sighed. "Lisi, you've really changed."

Well that one *totally* caught me off guard. The accusation was way more absurd than talking about the gerbil!

"Wait. *I've* changed? How can you even say that? You're the one who's gotten all weird and trendy and mean and I didn't even do anything!"

"Oh, so you think I'm not allowed to be trendy or something?" Mo asked, tugging at her skirt to straighten it. "Like you've got the market cornered?" She rolled her eyes angrily.

"No, that's not at *all* what I was trying to say! I just mean you're like a different person, and I feel like I didn't do anything to deserve how you've been acting toward me."

"You mean, me not fawning all over you? I'm so sick of your whole 'oh, I didn't do anything' act. You are *not* that helpless, Lisi. Really, how can you be so oblivious?" Mo shook her head like *I* was the crazy one. "It's not like life just, like, *happens* to you. You make your own fate. You choose what you do. Like trying to steal Jacqueline's boyfriend. Are you saying that's an *accident*?"

"Mo! They aren't even dating anymore! I mean, are they?" I dropped my voice down a notch or two and stepped closer to Mo. "And I'm not trying to steal Brett. We were just talking."

"Right. *Talking*. That's not exactly what it looked like when we came in here. You are so full of it, Lisi. I can't believe you would lie — and to my face."

"But I'm not lying! I never lied to you, Mo. Never!"

"Oh, so you mean there *is* going to be a celebrity guest at the kissing booth? Provided by your dad's *extensive* collection of famous contacts?" Mo had one hand on a hip, and her tone dripping with sarcasm.

"Well, no, but —"

"Right, so you're going to tell me that rumor just started itself, then?" Mo demanded, cutting me off. "It's a lie and you know it! And besides that, hitting on Brett, even if he and Jackie *did* break up, is still totally déclassé."

"You know what, Mo? I don't need this. I don't need you criticizing everything about me now that you have such great, cool, *popular*, perfect friends. Seriously." I could feel all the anger and frustration rising in my throat, strangling me.

I pushed on. "Just because you got back from Paris and decided to become a total poseur who ditches her old friends in order to 'broaden your social horizons' doesn't mean you have a right to be completely nasty. Or at least it doesn't mean I have to stand here and take it."

Mo's mouth had dropped open. "What do you mean, broaden my horizons?"

"Mo, I *saw* Johnny's interview with you, okay? I didn't mean to but we took the DVD we thought — well, anyway we watched the wrong one. I saw everything you said. Bella and I both saw. So I *know* all about your little plan to ditch us. What I fail to understand, though, is *why*. And you know what? Frankly, I don't care anymore. I'm sick of trying so hard to get along with everyone, when everybody acts like my own feelings don't matter."

"What feelings? Oh, right, those feelings you never actually *tell* anyone about."

"What do you mean?" I asked. It was my turn to be taken aback.

"Oh, come on, Lisi. You aren't exactly an open book. I have known you our whole lives and yet you rarely share your most personal thoughts." Mo looked at me almost pityingly. "It's like only your amazing wise older sister can know your secrets. Well, how is that supposed to make your so-called *friends* feel? And speaking of friends . . ." Mo raised her eyebrows and nodded her chin toward the door to the backyard.

I turned. In the doorway stood Johnny, holding his camera. It looked like it was off, thank goodness.

Mo went on. "Does *he* know you stole his DVD to watch my *confidential* interview?"

"What's she talking about?" Johnny asked, running his free hand through his wavy dark hair and looking at me, then Mo, then me again.

I hadn't thought that I could feel any lower than I already did. Until now. It was like I was plummeting down a dark well, my heart full of stones.

"Why don't you ask good old honest Lisi?" Mo asked, before I had a chance to answer him. I could see Mo *knew* she was being mean, because then she blushed a little, patted her hair, and stomped out into the yard.

Johnny just stood still for a second, as though letting the air clear.

I was so shaken from the fight that I was glad for the silence. I knew I'd have trouble talking without my voice breaking. I was doing everything in my power not to burst into tears.

Not here.

Not in Brett Jacobson's kitchen.

In the silence, I heard a tiny squeak. I glanced over at the gerbil tank. The little guy was sniffing with his paws against the glass, like he wanted to get out.

"He doesn't even have a name," I muttered.

"What?" Johnny asked.

"I said, do you wanna get out of here?" There it was. My voice was breaking.

Johnny let the screen door close behind him. I hadn't noticed he'd been holding it open this whole time. "Yeah, sure," he said. "Do you know where Bella went?"

I shook my head. I looked down at my phone. No texts.

I sent another one:

HEADING OUT IN A FEW. U WANT TO COME?

"I guess she went after Mason, huh?" Johnny said, wandering toward the front hall. I followed him numbly.

"Yeah. I guess so," I mumbled, still glancing down at my phone. Finally it vibrated, and I read the text.

NO

I shrugged, feeling utterly defeated. "I wouldn't know," I added, but I don't think Johnny heard me.

I breathed a sigh of relief as I sank into the familiar-feeling front seat of Johnny's car. At last, some normalcy.

But not for long.

"So what was Mo yammering about back there?" Johnny asked, pulling out onto the road and keeping his focus ahead of him.

"Um," I said, stalling.

I looked at the old digital clock. It was 12:23. How had we spent three whole hours at that party?

"When?" I asked.

Johnny looked at me — an unreadable expression on his face. I couldn't tell if it was a bemused look or an annoyed look or some other look altogether. I just felt so *tired*.

He didn't say anything.

"About the DVD," I filled in. "Yeah." Might as well be direct. "Bella. And I. Sort of like borrowed one of your DVDs and started watching it. But then we immediately realized it was the wrong one and put it back. I promise, no damage was done."

"Really. No damage." Johnny stared at the road. "So you were actually hoping it was a different DVD?"

"Yeah," I breathed, relieved that he understood.

But I glanced to my left and saw that Johnny did not look content. Not at all.

He didn't say anything else.

We drove the rest of the way home in silence. When we got to my house, I thanked Johnny for the ride as I got out of the car. He just kind of shrugged. "Hey, I'm always there when people need rides." He still kept his eyes on the road, even though he was in park.

"Okay, well, thanks again," I said. Johnny was obviously upset about the DVD stealing episode. But just then, I couldn't do anything about it. I'd already tried to apologize. Now what I needed to do was go to bed and try to forget that this night had ever happened.

Chapter 21

Sunday, sometime . . .

I barely got out of bed all day Sunday except to eat take-out with Mom, who was in total frantic mode because her gallery opening at the Linerfeld was tomorrow.

For the first time in a long time, I decided not to recharge my cell. All I wanted to do was hibernate under the covers. I hadn't even bothered to try cleaning Claire's pretty dress and it lay discarded in her room on top of the silver sandals and the usual mess.

Instead, I curled up in bed with a pair of scissors and a stack of magazines. It was satisfying in a way to tear out pages, cut up people's faces, stare mindlessly at articles about makeup, breakups, clothes, love. Did people really think magazines could explain love?

Snip, snip, snip.

I cut out a photo of a girl standing in the rain, staring out over a bridge. Her hair was plastered to her face.

I studied her expression. Did she look like someone had broken her heart? Like her world was falling down around her?

I cut out some other images and rearranged them all over and over again. It was calming, meditative even. Usually I would tape or glue some of them together until it was a collage and then hang it on the inside of my closet door or somewhere. But leaving the sanctity of the bed, even to grab a roll of tape from Mom's studio, seemed almost more than I could bear. So eventually I just lay down amid all the cut-ups and stared at the ceiling. I was too tired to cry. Too defeated.

At some point in the afternoon, I was lying under my cream-colored duvet, thinking of how Mo and I used to hide under the covers in her parents' bedroom, making a fort out of the blankets, and play with Mo's cat, Samson. Samson loved the tent game. I was recalling how Mo would chatter at Samson in a funny accent whenever we were inside the blanket tent, when I heard a knock on my bedroom door.

"Lis? I need your eye on something," I heard my mom creak open the bedroom door.

I stayed under the covers.

"No more sleeping, Lisi. I need you to look at a painting for me." My mom sounded as exhausted as I felt.

"Mom, go away," I said. Not meanly, at least I hoped. It was just that the idea of facing anyone after the disaster of last night was impossible. All I could do was replay my conversation with Brett and then with Mo over and over in my head.

Brett would be gone at the end of the year, and then what would I have to live for? I had been so used to hoarding away my crush on him. Now it was really just a matter of weeks until he graduated. And we were only just starting to get close! Not only did he know my name and my favorite kind of ice cream, but it was, like, every time I was around, he wanted to open up to me, tell me about his family, his struggles, his plans. It was, like, he somehow implicitly trusted me.

Was it because he knew how I felt about him? But how could he — unless he'd simply intuited it. Was I that obvious? No, I had to believe it was something more than that. We had a connection whenever we were around each other. I could feel it. He must feel it, too.

And that must be why he sent me that anonymous Facebook smooch. It *had* to have been him!

The idea filled me with elation, but I was still full of bitter frustration and confusion.

Because, if there *was* something between me and Brett, then why had he walked off with Jacqueline the minute she'd appeared?

All I knew was that Spring Carnival was Friday afternoon — less than one week away — and hopefully my questions would be answered.

* * *

Monday at school, I tried my best to lie low for most of the morning. I asked my mom to give me a ride so I wouldn't have to talk to Johnny or Bella until I'd fully emerged from my temporary social coma. My mom had been kind of surprised by the request but had gotten into the car in her paint-splattered silk pajamas without any questions asked.

For the first few periods, it seemed to be working: I managed to go from class to class without any conversations other than the occasional academic participation. Maybe it was the Monday morning dreariness, but there weren't as many random waves and smiles from strangers, like there had been at the end of last week. Instead, people simply looked at me curiously, and I looked away.

Posters and banners advertising all of the Spring Carnival events, however, still covered the walls and lockers and hung precariously over doorways. Little flyers littered the floors with ads for things like the fencing team's demo. I noted more than one freshman still handing out ChapSticks and breath mints, on which we'd glued little homemade stickers that said "Get smooched!"

Unfortunately, my anonymity didn't last past third period, when Timmy Reynolds bumped into me on the second-floor hall outside the bio department's horticulture room, just as I was rounding the corner. Timmy seemed convinced he'd seen me dancing on the coffee table at Brett's party on Saturday. Which was funny since I hadn't even seen Timmy at the party at all. And the last thing I needed was *more* rumors flying around.

Then, invariably, Timmy asked me if it was true that there was going to be a celebrity guest at the kissing booth on Friday.

I froze, trying to decide how to respond. I didn't know Timmy very well, only that he was on student council and occasionally stood on the stage during assemblies along with the class presidents, doing nothing of interest or importance. Basically, he was a hanger-on.

I *could* tell him the truth. That the whole celebrity appearance thing was a lie. But now at least half the school had heard about it. And what would Bella do if I started calling her out on her lie, publicly? No, we'd already discussed this. I couldn't go back on my word, even if it meant a little false advertising. I needed to stick to Bella's "plan."

And speaking of Bella, I had four text messages and two voice mails from her when I finally turned my phone on again this morning. They were all about the party, but she hadn't given any details of where she'd gone off to. I'd felt a flicker of jealousy in my chest. I was angry with Bella for disappearing at the party, leaving me to fend for myself, and totally failing to rescue me when I was under attack. But I was also glad for her if she *had* gotten together with Mason. It's just that it was unfair. Things were always working out for Bella and some boy. Anyone she wanted to kiss, or just flirt with, she had no problem making it happen. Mason had been her first real challenge, but apparently he wasn't *that* much of a challenge in the end, and I almost felt disappointed that despite all of Bella's agonizing, he hadn't been that hard to get after all.

By then, Timmy had given up and wandered off. I hoped he'd taken my silence as an affirmative, or the exact opposite.

The one thing I felt I could still hope for was that Brett had meant what he said on Saturday night. That he thought the kissing booth was cool. That he knew I was going to be there. All of that must have meant that he had at least *considered* being there, too. It almost didn't matter about anything else. If I could finally lose my NBK status to Brett, it seemed like every other problem I ever had would just solve itself.

I was thinking this very thought as I opened the second-floor girls' bathroom door and entered, only to find Jacqueline and Cindy Ramirez at one of the sinks.

Cindy was adjusting her bra straps so that they would show on purpose out of the sides of her little yellow cap-sleeved T-shirt. Jacqueline was drawing pale pink lip liner around her lips.

I wanted to slink back out of the bathroom and use the one near the caf instead . . . but it was too late. Jacqueline saw me in the mirror, pouted, and put down the liner.

"Just ignore her," Cindy muttered — but not too quietly. She rolled her eyes at me as I inched in. My plan was to grab a paper towel and then immediately leave. Peeing could not happen when enemies were lurking.

But apparently Jacqueline had another idea in mind. "So, Lisi," she said, still talking to my reflection in the mirror rather than turning to face me. "Did you enjoy the party Saturday?" Her tone was strange, like she was referring to an inside joke that I didn't get.

I decided to play it cool. "Yeah, it was fine." I shrugged, for added effect.

"It was *fiiine*," Cindy mimicked in a high-pitched voice.

Oh god. This was not going to work. I made a lunge for the paper towel dispenser, just as Jacqueline turned to Cindy and said, "Some girls just don't know how to play at their own level."

Cindy laughed a chirping laugh. "Seriously," she agreed.

"And girls like that should know when they're playing with fire."

"Right," Cindy said.

I grabbed the paper towel and tried to leave, but Jacqueline swiveled away from the mirror and looked me in the eye.

"You should know that if you try and get with Brett Jacobson, you will seriously regret it. Take it from me," she said, her head tilted, like she was just giving me some helpful advice. But there was an evil gleam in her eye. Was she threatening me?

"Thanks for the warning," I said coolly. "I'll try to remember that when I win the Spring Carnival prize."

And then I shoved open the door and left it swinging shut in Jacqueline's face.

My heart was racing as I marched down the hallway toward the cafeteria. I was both terrified and totally charged by my confrontation with Jacqueline in the bathroom. It felt *so* good to put her in her place. At the same time, I wasn't prepared to go up against the most popular girl in my school. And now I knew for sure it was war.

I needed my friends. I needed them on my side to deal with this. We had to prove that the kissing booth really could win. We *had* to, if we didn't want to end up the biggest fools of all. I vowed to myself to apologize again to Johnny about how we stole his DVD. I'd figure out some way to make it up to him. Then I'd ask Bella all about her night on Saturday, and I'd will myself to be happy for her and not jealous.

But I was in for another surprise when Bella threw her cottage cheese and seltzer lunch onto our table in the caf and asked me point blank:

"Since when do you have a crush on Brett?"

This was definitely not good. This was, in fact, very very bad. *Had Mo told her? Did everyone know now?*

"Well?" Bella prodded, ripping open her cottage cheese carton vigorously.

"Shhhh," I said. Johnny was approaching.

"Oh, so your feelings for Brett are a secret from *all* your friends. Well, good, at least I'm not the only one who was out of the loop." Bella dived into eating her cottage cheese with an annoyed look on her face.

Out of nowhere I suddenly felt tears forming. "Can we not talk about this right now?" I whispered.

Johnny was standing next to the table, but he had obviously heard the whole exchange. Great. It was out. They knew.

But really, they couldn't be *that* mad at me, could they?

Apparently they could. Johnny didn't even put down the bottle of Coke he was holding. "You know what?" he said. "I just realized I have to send out some more demos. I've been meaning to keep up more with my mailings." Johnny rarely did his mailings at school. Plus, he already told me on Friday that he'd done a mailing.

"I'm just gonna head to the library," he now said, "and, uh, get some of that stuff done. No time like the present and all that jazz."

"Have fun." Bella shrugged and opened her seltzer water. I watched him saunter off. He didn't look back once, not to smirk or anything. Great.

"So," Bella said. "When were you planning to tell me?"

"Bella," I said in a hoarse whisper. "It's not like that. It's no big deal. I just flirted with him a little at the party. Nothing happened."

"So how long have you liked him? Since before my crush on Mason?"

"Um . . ."

"Since before winter break?"

"Well . . ."

Bella put her spoon down. "No way. You're totally obsessed with him, aren't you? God. I KNEW IT."

"You did?" I couldn't help feeling a surge of excitement and relief alongside my embarrassment. "How did you know?"

"Lisi. We've been best friends for a long time. I thought you *trusted* me." Bella folded her arms, kind of like Mo had done Saturday night.

"I *did*! I mean I *do*. It's just. I didn't tell anyone. Seriously, Bells. No one. Well, except for Mo. But no one else. It's not a big deal. I mean it's one of those pointless things where it's like there was never any chance of anything happening so what would have been the reason to bring it up?" I felt really squirmy and uncomfortable. It was too hot for my sweater, but taking it off seemed too complicated.

"Oh, I dunno, maybe because it's important to you? And what's important to you is also important to your friends? I can't believe you told Mo and not me."

I didn't know what to say. Bella's accusation was oddly similar to what Mo had said to me at the party.

"Lisi," she went on. "All this time. You should've just told me. I could have helped you!"

"Do what?"

"It doesn't matter. Anything. Besides, I'm always telling *you* stuff." I couldn't tell if Bella was truly mad.

"Yeah, but I have nothing to tell," I insisted. "I keep *saying*, nothing happened Saturday. What I want to know is what happened with *you*. Did you hang out with Mason?"

Bella shrugged. "Maybe."

"Oh, come on, Bella, just tell me."

"Why should I?"

"Bella."

"No, really, Lisi. Tell me why I should tell you." She was obviously not going to let me off easy.

"Um, because . . . well, because I talked to my dad again yesterday. And, like, he said we're good."

For the second time, Bella dropped her spoon. "We're good? As in, celebrity appearance good?"

"Yup!" I lied. Why was I lying? Oh my God. But since everyone was so hot on accusing me of not telling the truth these days, I figured I might as well do just that.

"Who who WHO?" Bella asked, bouncing up and down in her seat.

"Shhh!" I leaned over the table, partly to keep our conversation hidden and partly because I didn't feel like I could support myself upright. Lying made my head hurt. "Dad told me I can't say who it is. Just in case."

At least now, I reasoned, I would still have one friend.

"Is this for real?" Bella asked, clearly still impressed.

"You said yourself, Bells. Once Dad asked around, it was easy."

"Easy," Bella repeated, a smile widening across her face.

"Yup," I nodded, looking down at my sandwich and suddenly feeling very unhungry. "Easy."

Chapter 22

Tuesday, 7 p.m.

The next night, my dad was humming the new iMac commercial song loudly in the bathroom as he tied his tie. Occasionally he'd break from standard humming to "dah-dah dah dah dah-dah dah-dah dah dah dah"-ing. I considered telling my dad I didn't feel well and should probably stay home tonight, but I knew how crushed my mother would be.

Mom was already at the gallery making sure everything was set up properly.

I shut my history book — yellow journalism would have to wait — and tugged on a black wrap shirt, black skirt, and sheer black tights. I stepped in front of my mirror. I looked like I was going to a funeral. But wasn't black what you were supposed to wear to artistic events?

Twenty minutes later, my dad and I were parking along the side of the curb. I was impressed to see a line of other cars along the street and filling the small lot that adjoined the gallery building. I felt a surge of pride in my mom. I had no idea people really came to gallery openings — I guess I had been too young to ever see one of my mother's shows.

Inside, the place was drafty, and people milled about slowly, examining the four large Cecilia Newton paintings delivered to the building on Sunday. I wasn't sure what I had imagined, but this was really nice — the gallery consisted of one large room with high vaulted ceilings at the front. Three of my mom's paintings hung on the back wall and one particularly wide canvas was on one of the side walls. On another wall was a table with plates of crackers and cubed cheese and some bottles of wine. My mother was talking to a woman in a suit and nodding her head vigorously.

The crowd was mostly adults, and I wandered around aimlessly for a while until someone tapped on my shoulder.

"Lisi!"

"Oh, hi, Mrs. Dean!"

It was Cora, Mo's mom. I hadn't seen her in over a month. My stomach felt like it had fallen somewhere down around my knees.

"We haven't seen you in at least a month! How are you doing?"

"Oh, I was just thinking the same thing." I smiled. Polite convo with your former best friend's parent was the worst.

"Have you seen Molly? She's right over there by the cheese and crackers. Go on and say hi," Cora said, shooing me in Mo's direction.

I had no choice. I approached Mo, the *Jaws* theme song playing in my head.

"Hey."

"Hey."

"They have Swiss." Molly stuck a piece of cheese into her mouth. She chewed with her mouth slightly open, like she always had.

"Yeah." I stood there and watched Mo eat the piece of cheese. "So hey, Mo," I went on. "Listen. I'm sorry about Saturday. I mean, I don't really understand what happened, but I'm really sorry if I offended you or did something to make you mad."

Mo stopped chewing her cheese and sighed. "It's okay. I mean, it's just life. Sometimes friends just stop being right for each other."

"I guess," I said sadly. It was hard realizing what she meant. Had we really grown apart that much? When had that happened? I still felt like I didn't understand what had changed between us.

"So. How's life?" Mo asked. I could tell she really was curious about how I was doing. I could see it in her eyes when she finally looked at me.

"It's cool," I said, "You know. In the sense that my

world is falling down around me and there's nothing I can do about it. I mean, not to be melodramatic."

Mo shrugged. "I don't know why you're going along with Bella's lie about this whole special-guest nonsense."

"Wait, how did you know Bella made it all up?"

"Um, hello. Kind of obvious. I've known you two forever. Doesn't take a rocket scientist."

I let out my breath. I hadn't realized I'd been holding it. "It wouldn't have been so bad, if —" I blurted, and then stopped myself. Should I really be confiding in Mo? Was she the one who gave away my secret about Brett? Could she really be trusted?

". . . if the most popular girl in school hadn't decided to make you her direct competition for winning the Spring Carnival prize? Yeah, kinda sucks to be you right now," Mo finished my sentence for me and ate another piece of cheese. She looked at me sympathetically.

At least she wasn't angry anymore, like she had been Saturday night.

"Yeah," I sighed. "The most popular girl in school who also happens to be *your* new bestie. Why exactly are you now friends with Jacqueline, again? It just seemed so, like, sudden. One minute everything was normal. Then you get back from spring break and it's a total social changeover. It's one thing to grow apart . . . and I mean you can look and act however you want, I'm just wondering what brought about the change? And *more importantly* — why Jacqueline?"

"You wouldn't get it, Lisi."

"Try me."

Mo raised her eyebrows. "I guess I just understood her."

"Ugh, who can understand a girl like that. Everything just falls into her lap all the time." I rolled my eyes and poked at the doily sticking out of the cheese tray.

"That's not true," Mo said indignantly. "She was seriously sad about breaking up with Brett."

"Really? Do you know what actually *happened* between them?" If I had antennae on my head, they'd be waving around, sensing important information in the air.

Mo shrugged. "I don't know the whole story. But she was definitely sad. She said it was really hard to have to lose someone you thought you had feelings for, feelings that were, like, real."

"And you felt sorry for her?" I asked, totally confused.

"Well, I just *got* what she was going through."

"I'm not following," I said. "How did you get what she was going through? You've never broken up with anyone."

And then, all of a sudden, things started to fall into place. "Hold it. Wait. Are you keeping something from me? Does this involve a boy?"

Now it was Mo's turn to look sheepish.

"*Who?*" I asked. I had picked up a cheese cube but

immediately dropped it back onto the tray. "Come on," I prodded. "Now that you know all of my secrets, can't you share yours? If I promise not to tell?"

Mo looked at me skeptically, then leaned in. "Promise not to make fun of me?" Mo asked.

"Duh!" I assured her.

"PS?"

I hooked my pinky finger into hers for a pinky swear.

"Johnny," Mo said.

"Where? I didn't think he was coming tonight," I said, looking around to see what Mo was referring to.

But I didn't see Johnny anywhere.

Then I looked back at Mo and saw how red her face was. And that's when I realized.

"Johnny? *JOHNNY?*" I scrunched my eyebrows together and looked hard at Mo to see whether she was joking.

"So here's the thing," Mo said, blushing all over. "When I was in Paris I decided I was going to tell him when I got back that I liked him."

I felt like I would need a crane to get my jaw off the floor.

"You LIKED Johnny?"

Mo reddened more but kept talking. "I ended up waiting until we were alone, which ended up being right before my interview with him. You know, for his film and stuff."

In a way, I could tell Mo was kind of relieved to get all of this off her chest. And I was too fascinated by it all to stop and think about the logic of it.

"And?" I prodded.

"*And.* He told me he wasn't interested. Because he likes someone else. End of story. Game over."

"And *that's* the reason you stopped hanging out with us, and started hanging out with Jacqueline?"

Mo was still blushing. "See, I knew you wouldn't get it. When the person you like tells you they like someone else, it's not exactly the easiest thing in the world to get over. I just . . . needed some space," Mo admitted guiltily. "And Jacqueline understood!"

"But back up. Really? Did you really like Johnny?"

Mo turned a deeper shade of red, and nodded.

"And he liked someone else?"

She nodded.

I was still totally shocked.

"But there's one thing I just don't get." I stared at Mo, confused. "Who's this mysterious other girl that Johnny likes?"

A strange look passed over Mo's face.

"No idea," she said. "It could be anyone."

Chapter 23

Wednesday, 10 a.m.

Anyone?

I glanced around as I headed from gym to bio the next day.

Anyone at all?

It seemed crazy to think that there was some girl roaming around that Johnny was secretly in love with. Did EVERYONE have secret crushes? And I had thought we all knew everything we needed to know about each other.

This week had shown me the exact opposite was true.

Was it Katrina?

No way.

Celeste?

Impossible.

Some sort of nondescript girl who nonetheless

always seemed to be everywhere at once? Like Petra Wu? I just couldn't get my head around it.

Suddenly, I stopped walking as certainty thudded into my stomach. I stopped so abruptly in fact that some scrawny boy behind me stumbled and dropped a textbook. I didn't even bother to help him pick it up. Because at that very second, Trish the Traitor was standing at the corner between the front office and the language hall, handing out little pins. When I approached her, Trish looked sheepish as she put a pin into my palm. It said BE FLY. I walked away like a zombie, staring at the pin in my hand.

What if it was Trish? What if Trish was the mystery girl Johnny liked?

The idea sent a chill down my spine. I threw the pin in the Dumpster out by the back lot.

I had to stop thinking about this. I had other problems to worry about.

The rest of Wednesday and then Thursday seemed to go by in slow motion. As unmoored as I felt, I had to admit my popularity had never been higher. It was like everyone thought I was the new "champion of the underdog," that I represented the voice of all the kids who had privately harbored resentment toward Jacqueline and her crew for as long as they had been at the top of the social food chain — i.e., forever.

People were coming up to me and congratulating me for the "showdown" between me and Jacqueline Saturday night. I had figured out quickly that saying something like "what showdown?" was generally received with a knowing wink — the rumors didn't seem to need any actual confirmation to be considered the truth. By some accounts, Jacqueline and I had smeared frosting from a birthday cake on each other. Others believed Jacqueline had caught me kissing Brett and had punched me. (Hello, no bruises, people!)

Some said both of us had left the party crying. And there were even more extreme stories floating around from what I could tell, involving a skinny-dipping scenario, the cops, a rubber ducky (huh?), and a whole other assortment of details that made absolutely no sense whatsoever. But one thing was clear: Everyone knew that I was now the big new threat to the reigning queen. And everyone knew the competition all came down to what was going to happen at Spring Carnival.

Would the Fly Girls beat the kissing booth? Would there be a celebrity appearance — and if so, who would it be? And which girl would come out on top?

For the first time ever, everyone wanted to know me. And all I wanted was to disappear. To be left alone to think. And to dread. Because I alone knew the real outcome of the Spring Carnival. Which was that the kissing booth coordinators would all be exposed as frauds for making up a schoolwide lie. And everyone would find out that I was an NBK freak. Brett would never think twice about me again — and then he'd be gone for good. And then the school year would be over, and I would go join a nunnery somewhere in the Alps and forget all of this had ever happened.

Or something very similar to all that.

Thursday night, my feeling of utter doom must have been visible from several miles away, because even my father — who was usually not actually present, and when he was, was hardly ever *mentally* present — noticed it right away.

"What's going on, Sugar Bug?" he asked me as I dropped my backpack on the front stairs and sank down next to it. He was standing in the foyer, sorting through the mail.

"What are you doing home so early?" I asked in reply. I dimly remembered my mom saying she'd be checking out the gallery space tonight, so I figured I'd have the place to myself and could wallow in peace. No such luck.

"Just sealed a pretty big deal. Everyone left early to celebrate. Figured we'd start the real work on it tomorrow. But hey, I asked you first," he said, waving an envelope at me.

"Hm. I guess you could say I sealed a deal, too, this week."

Sealed the deal on my fate as a spinster, I thought.

"Anything I can help with?" Dad asked.

"Unless you can get Lindsay Lohan or Brad Pitt on the phone, I seriously doubt it."

"I told you what happened when they wanted Lindsay to do the Noxzema campaign," Dad answered distractedly.

I sighed and kicked my flip-flops off, leaning back on my elbows on the step behind me.

"Well," Dad continued, looking at me seriously. "I wish I could help on the celebrity front. But since I can't, you'll want to grab some socks."

"Socks?" My dad rarely made any sense.

"I think you'll be glad you did," he answered. "And hurry — I'll be waiting in the car."

I gave him another curious look, but he seemed serious and was already turning to head back out the front door. So I ran upstairs, grabbed some socks, put on my flip-flops, and then met him in the car.

"Where are we going?" I asked, clutching my balled-up pair of socks as he pulled out onto the main drive. But he told me I'd see soon enough, and I finally figured it out when we pulled into the parking lot at Majestic Lanes.

"Seriously, Dad? Bowling?" I stretched my arms as I got out of the car. A paper sign was taped to the front door that said WEDNESDAY HAPPY HOUR 5–9, THURSDAY LADIES NITE, FRIDAY 80S NITE.

I couldn't remember the last time I'd been to Majestic. Probably not since eighth-grade graduation week. The entire grade had gone, and we'd gotten in trouble when Ken Roberts — who moved away after that year — ran down the gutter and threw his math book at the pins, putting one of the lanes out of service.

Majestic Lanes was pretty deserted for a Thursday night. A group of middle-aged ladies were gathered at one end, laughing uproariously. I suspected they were drunk. It was weird to think of grown-ups getting drunk like that. It was also deeply mortifying to be bowling with my father on "Ladies Nite." But I knew I didn't have a choice — such was the nature of Dad's spontaneous decisions — and anyway, I was relieved that at least there were no kids from my school around to witness the scene. And frankly, I was grateful for something to keep me busy.

Because the Spring Carnival was tomorrow. My stomach had been in knots all day. Tomorrow was the beginning of the end of my life. Just thinking about it now made me a little dizzy as I sat down to tie on my bowling shoes. Or maybe that was just the multicolored flashing lights over the lanes.

Anyone could see Cliff Jared was having far more fun at the bowling alley than his daughter.

For one thing, his score hovered about ninety points above mine for the majority of the game. He had gotten several strikes and had invented a little victory dance that would have been embarrassing in normal circumstances. I knew he was just trying to lift my spirits. But since my entire social life was in ruins and about to be one hundred million times worse when the boy of my dreams found out I was a big lying loser, relatively speaking, my dad's dancing wasn't all that horrible to suffer through.

The weird thing was, though, that as much as I'd been obsessing inwardly about Brett for going on three years, it wasn't what occupied my thoughts the most tonight.

What bore down on me instead was the fact that my best friends had all been hiding things from me. And I'd been hiding from them, too — so I couldn't really hold it against them. But it was so disorienting, like finding out the sky was actually green, and grass, blue.

I couldn't decide what was weirder — that Molly used to have a crush on Johnny, or that Johnny apparently liked someone else, and none of us knew who. I could understand Mo's side of it. Johnny was a great guy. He was super smart. He was funny. Now that I really thought about it, I realized Johnny was good-looking in a sort of slightly grungier Casey Affleck way. Even his wrinkly old T-shirts with esoteric sayings had an endearing quality.

The main thing about him that was so great, though, was just how he could make you feel. Whenever I was around Johnny, I felt like I was comfortable being myself. Around him, it was easy to believe that I was a funny and interesting person, not just some boring girl who'd never been kissed.

And in every Johnny conversation, there was just this sense of sinking into something that felt right.

So yeah, I could definitely understand what Mo would see in Johnny. But what I couldn't fathom was that Johnny, who always seemed so face value — who always kept it real and spoke his mind freely — had hidden this huge thing from all of us. It just didn't seem like him to be secretive.

Yes, he was private when it came to his film work. But having a secret crush was a whole other ball game. I had thought that *I* had the market cornered on that.

Turns out I couldn't have been more naive. Everyone kept their truest feelings to themselves.

The realization made me feel strange and cold all over.

"Yoohoo! I said it's your turn, Lis." My dad handed me one of the bowling balls, and I felt my whole body hunch over with the weight of it as I stood up to play my turn.

But why hadn't Johnny told me and Bella about what had happened with Mo? Especially after Mo started acting so mean toward us, I couldn't figure out why Johnny hadn't mentioned what was going on. I supposed Mo had begged him to keep it confidential. And if there was one thing Johnny was good for, it was holding up his end of a promise.

Still. Something about the whole story just didn't fit together, and I was wrestling with all these thoughts as I leaned back, swung out, and set the ball rolling down the shiny, wax-polished lane.

I was astonished to see all of the pins wobbling, falling.

Then there was just one pin left standing.

And I knew.

I suddenly in that moment understood why all of this was bothering me so much. Why I couldn't understand how brilliant, cute, witty, goofy Johnny — Johnny who had always been there for me — Johnny who stared at me with his intense dark eyes, who chased me around and made me laugh and ruffled my hair in the halls and called me on Friday nights just to kill the time — how *that* Johnny could like someone else.

I couldn't understand it because I wanted him to like *me*.

But what did this mean for my crush on Brett? Was it all an illusion?

Of course I still thought Brett was hot. And mysterious. And that I saw something in him which no one else saw.

And besides, Brett had sent me the anonymous smooch.

I still wanted to kiss Brett at the kissing booth. How could I not? That was still my goal.

And yet.

When there's just one pin left standing, you start to

see things a little more clearly. When it really came down to it, the thought of Johnny liking Trish or some other mystery girl, well, I just could *not* stand for that.

There had to be something I could do.

Before it was too late.

Chapter 24

Friday, 12p.m.

All morning there was chaos: chaos when I first woke up groggy from so much tossing and turning, couldn't find anything to wear, tripped over the silver sandals, and hit my elbow on the edge of the vanity. Then chaos during homeroom when they announced over the loud-speaker that classes would end at noon and everyone cheered and the cheering turned into mass running around, collecting of carnival supplies and just general mayhem. Chaos in the halls between classes as people made last-ditch attempts to promote their booths, prepare for the fair, or just ran around (again) excitedly. Even the alterna-anarchist-goths were feeling rowdy — who doesn't love a half day of classes, a chance to be outside in the springtime?

By the time noon rolled around, it was all I could do to remain upright. I was tired from lack of sleep, and the anxiety of what was going to happen (or *not* going to happen) was giving me serious hideous under-eye baggage.

I had searched through Claire's closet several times that morning but finally ended up deciding on an outfit from my own. It felt like the beginning of the new me, and I had to start somewhere even if it was as simple as wearing my own clothes for once, instead of hiding behind Claire's wardrobe. I'd forgotten about this white dress with flowers on it that I had. It was flirty and springy — the perfect thing for Spring Carnival.

And on the night of Brett's party, Johnny had said I should wear dresses more.

My hair, on the other hand, was a wild nightmare. I'd had to wrestle it back into little side ponytails and just hope for the best.

The chaos of the day was made worse by the fact that the Fly Girls had been prancing about all morning, practically begging people to sign up for their Dance Dance Revolution dance contest and handing out all kinds of items covered in the words *Be Fly*. Even *I* imagined, if circumstances were different, that the dance booth sounded like it could be kind of fun.

I was thinking these traitorous thoughts as I pushed through the gym doors and out to the soccer field, after showing my school ID to Mrs. Vargo, the school secretary. Inside the gym was where you signed in, bought as many tickets as you wanted, pledged donations, and showed your ID or guest pass before entering the Spring

Carnival. The entire carnival was contained in our school's two playing fields and surrounded on all sides by a chain-link fence that had several guarded exits.

As soon as I stepped outside, I immediately felt a powerful surge of hope and excitement.

The smell of fertilizer hit me like it always did, but this time it was overpowered by the smell of cotton candy, buttery popcorn, and baked goods. I squinted into the sun and adjusted my dress, feeling jittery, like I'd just slurped down an espresso. My classmates were streaming out of the school doors and headed toward the playing field as well. I stopped walking and stood there, shielding my eyes from the sun with my hand as people rushed past me on either side.

In the distance, a huge Ferris wheel had been carted onto the lower field and stood there looking still and empty. Everyone was in setup mode, putting the finishing touches on their booths, blowing up balloons, filling nets with plastic balls, lining up apples, hanging signs.

Our two adjacent playing fields were both overtaken by rides and booths. The booths were set up in rows across most of the upper part, East Field, except for a clearing right in the middle that allowed room for a mini-stage, where a band was setting up.

I saw The Gross Man, assistant principal, pacing the makeshift stage, shouting orders to some guys who were securing speakers. He looked like he was in his usual frenzy. Members of the boys' chorus were holding sheet music and doing warm-ups behind the stage. They were dressed as pirates, complete with tights. No joke. They always opened the act, then usually there would be a slightly cooler school band, and then the main show would be some way more hip band — no one famous or anything, but we'd had some cool performances from indie Chicago groups in the past.

As I wandered closer, the boys' chorus took the stage and began performing some kind of "seafaring" song that got drowned out by all the shouting and laughter.

Lower down, the West Field was dominated on the left by all the rides — the Ferris wheel, a Gravitron, plus one of those giant swing rides. On the other end of the West Field was where the thirty-foot movie screen hung, and a handful of other booths were lined up on either side of it.

I was supposed to be at the kissing booth already, helping with the setup. But I took my time, weaving through the crowd, taking it all in. Most of the action closest to the entrance through the gym consisted of snack stands. I saw snow cones, cotton candy, jumbo pretzels, and a Miss Daisy's Mexican stand. A lot of the language clubs had set up booths nearby with themed food, the most popular being the Italian Club's hoagies and pizza. Judson Green raced past me, two Twizzlers hanging out of his nostrils. The kid could NOT go anywhere without putting things up his nose.

As I made my way down the next aisle of booths, I saw people getting caricatures drawn by the Art

Club, and others getting their faces painted. I saw Trish and her two friends in line for the face painting. Relief and happiness flooded me temporarily when I saw that Johnny was not with them.

The karaoke booth was also in action, with a huge line of people waiting to sing their hearts out in front of the entire school. Dave Hallston was currently belting "We Are the Champions," but it sounded more like an animal dying a painful death. Of course, since Dave Hallston was one of the Populars, girls were screaming and cheering for him. I noticed Mason in the crowd but didn't see Brett.

Pie throwing and the dunk tank also drew big crowds. Mr. Lory was the first teacher to sit in the dunk tank and I noticed Ms. Lewis, the new girls' basketball coach, helping some girls perfect their aim. I thought about Johnny's comment on the possible affair between Mr. Lory and Ms. Lewis, how he saw them as vital side characters in the social drama of high school.

A few kids had broken into the supply shed next to the gym and were pushing stolen scooters around. One kid was just running in circles with a badminton racket, hollering like a lunatic. It was amazing what a little freedom could turn into! Meanwhile, in the distance I saw that the line for the Ferris wheel had started forming, and as the first batch of kids got on, it squealed into motion.

The funniest thing I passed was the Young Republicans booth. It consisted of four boys, all of whom wore glasses and surly expressions. I recognized one of the boys as Jason from my history class, the one who dressed and acted like a miniature forty-year-old. They were trying to get people to sign some kind of petition. They'd made a big banner out of someone's old blue bedsheet and had glued cardboard letters to it. But as anyone who'd *ever* used glue before could have predicted, the fabric was not exactly holding.

I couldn't help giggling a little deliriously when I saw their sign. It was clear that foul play had gone on. What had originally spelled out YOUNG REPUBLICANS had been tampered with and now simply read:

YOU R PUBIC

Nice. *Classy.*

I wished Johnny was around to witness, and hoped he would have a chance to catch it on camera before the Young R's noticed what had happened. For a second I wondered if Johnny was already at the kissing booth, helping out. Or was he perhaps going after his Mystery Girl at that very moment?

I shook my head and made my way more quickly toward the West Field, my heart rate picking up. The end of the West Field was where Celeste had told us all to gather. We had analyzed prime locations and decided that setting up not far from the big movie projection screen gave us a sort of destination-point advantage, setting us apart from all the other booths on the East Field.

Apparently, though, the Fly Girls had had the same

idea, because they were setting up their booth directly across from us. I heard screaming and saw Jacqueline, Cindy, and some other Fly Girls dashing by, waving their arms. Members of the football team ran in front of them jeering and laughing. I made my way around a big hot dog stand to see what all the commotion was about, and saw that the football team had apparently snatched the Fly Girls' skirts and were wearing them over their uniforms. The Fly Girls were left in only their little mini-shorts, which was kind of embarrassing. Then the Fly Girls caught up with the football players and tackled them, trying to get their skirts back. The whole scene quickly turned into a hormone-frenzied battle, and I couldn't help but notice Jacqueline flirting with one of the quarterbacks.

My walking had turned into a light jog. Then I saw Petra chatting with a girl at the Literacy Club's booth.

"Petra!" I shouted. She turned and smiled when she saw me approaching.

"Hey, Lisi!" She waved.

"Petra, aren't we supposed to be helping to set up?" I asked, panting a little.

"Oh yeah, definitely," she said, saying good-bye quickly to her friend. "Come on, let's go," she said, clearly reading the urgency on my face.

Together we started running toward the meeting place. I could see Celeste's bright red hair from afar. As we got closer, I saw Daniel and Sarah trying to erect Daniel's hand-built booth without it toppling over.

With its white and burgundy stripes glinting in the sun, it actually looked pretty impressive and professional. A cutely designed list of rules was posted to the side. My chest tightened when I saw the big sign attached to the booth, which said GET KISSED BY THE STARS! and another one that said DON'T MISS SPECIAL CELEBRITY GUEST APPEARANCE!

Everyone had been gossiping about who they thought the guest would be. But Bella had supported my "family privacy," saying that for professional reasons we still couldn't divulge the star's name.

Too bad the star didn't even exist.

But I was the only one who knew that.

Meanwhile, Celeste was directing everyone around. Bella was behind the booth, arranging the table. I felt another pang, knowing that once Bella found out that I had lied to her about the celebrity appearance, it would all be over. Bella would probably hate me almost as much as the rest of the school would.

I looked around, but I didn't see Johnny anywhere.

"THERE you guys are!" Bella exclaimed. "You know, just because your shifts didn't start yet doesn't mean you didn't have to help set up," she said, handing us each a ChapStick. She grabbed me by the arm and pulled me behind the booth. "So? Where's our guest? Any word?"

I panicked. A line was already starting to form. And I had a feeling they were all there because they expected to see a celebrity. But what could I do?

Sarah Singer began eagerly collecting tickets and stashing them in our designated cashbox as Celeste, Petra, and Dan took up the first shift. People took turns getting cheek kisses. Most of the guys gravitated toward Celeste. Clearly the girls in line were disappointed, waiting for the star appearance. But shockingly, there were a lot of girls who actually *wanted* to kiss Daniel the Dork.

"Um," I began, taking a step away from the booth. "I was just on the phone with my dad, actually . . ."

I saw Bella's eyes light up in anticipation. *How could I do this?* "And he said that they're . . . they're . . . they're on their way!"

"Eeee!" Bella squealed. Several people in the line started getting excited, too, clearly having overheard. More people started crowding around and waving their tickets.

I saw Mason in line. He had a half smile on his tan face and was looking right at Bella. "*So?*" I asked Bella, nodding toward Mason.

"Oh." She blushed. "Yeah. I guess I owe you. It turns out he thought I was hot all along — he just wasn't sure I'd want to settle down with one guy!"

"I wonder what would have given him THAT idea?" I smirked. But I was happy for her. At least she'd have Mason, then, when she ended our friendship.

All of a sudden, Celeste, who was not sitting behind the booth but had gotten in the line, began making out with Daniel. Whoa! Apparently she couldn't handle watching everyone else steal him from her. It was kind of funny actually, but causing a bit of mayhem at the booth.

Bella finally shouted, "Hey, no tongue and no touching. Read the rules," and pulled the two of them apart.

And then just as suddenly, Bella stopped squealing and flapping her arms and immediately straightened. She turned to me. "Lisi," she said in a strange tone.

"Huh?" *Did she know I was lying? Was this the end of it all?*

"It's your shift," Bella said quietly, then grabbed my arm and literally shoved me into the folding chair where Celeste had been sitting.

I had no idea why she was being so urgent about our change in shift . . . until I looked through the frame of the booth and out at the cluttered, crowded field.

And saw Brett.

He was walking over slowly, confidently, the sun dancing off of his light hair. As he got closer, he slowed down even more, one hand casually slung in the pocket of his slightly loose fitting jeans.

Finally, he was at the other side of the table. It was almost like the crowd had parted to let him through.

He held out a ticket to Sarah Singer, whose jaw dropped open a little. Everyone gathered around was all atwitter about the celebrity appearance that was supposed to happen any second. But many of them had taken notice of Brett's approach and were now watching us closely.

"Hey," I smiled. I couldn't help feeling triumphant. He had come. "So are you, like, here for Natalie Portman or whoever?"

"Nah," he said, shrugging. He ran his hand through his floppy hair.

"Oh," I breathed, wishing I had something to fan myself with. My stomach felt like it was turning over itself, like the gerbil wheel in Brett's kitchen, with a nameless gerbil running around inside it.

"Actually," he said, hunching down and resting one hand on the table. By now, even more people were focusing on our interaction, and I didn't know what to do.

Brett grinned mischievously. I noticed for the first time that his white teeth were kind of crooked. His grin was almost more menacing than sexy.

The blood hammered in my ears.

He leaned in. His breath was so close to my face I could feel it on my skin.

I closed my eyes. *This was it.*

He whispered: "I came here for you."

And then, like a bucket of cold water falling over my shoulders, I suddenly opened my eyes and jerked away from Brett.

I couldn't exactly say why, but I just couldn't let myself be a *fraud* any longer. I looked at Brett's flustered face and realized I felt nothing — that I hardly knew him. As much as I had wanted to kiss Brett — and to shake off my NBK status forever — it just didn't feel right.

After all, I had lied to him. To everyone. To myself.

I stood up in what felt like slow motion but must have actually been extremely quickly, because my chair went tumbling out from under me as I rose.

Brett leaned back a little with a startled look on his face. Clearly he wasn't used to being, well, rejected.

I grabbed my chair off the ground and set it back down where it was in plain view of the crowd. Then I climbed up and stood on top of it, staring out into the sea of expectant faces.

"EVERYBODY!" I shouted.

People quieted a little and I went on. "I have an announcement to make about the kissing booth!" I saw Bella raise her eyebrows at me, but I continued anyway.

I cleared my throat. "I have some unfortunate news. You see, there will be no celebrity guest. It was a lie. It's my fault. I didn't know how to let everyone down. I deceived all of you."

There was grumbling in the crowd but I pushed on. "The thing is, I thought I could hide my true intentions from everyone. It's easy to think you can protect yourself as long as you don't risk anything, as long as you keep your cards to yourself and don't let anyone else see the truth." People looked at me like I was insane, but I had to get this off my chest. It was now or never.

"I had a secret crush on somebody. And I ended up hiding it from everyone who was important to me, at the price of my closest friendships. Now, is that really worth it? Especially when you stop to think about it and realize that a secret crush is no more than a fantasy if you aren't willing to admit it aloud. Sometimes people grow apart. But that doesn't mean we should push them away. And what's more, I was ashamed of myself. I didn't want anyone to know that I had never been kissed." At this, more people in the crowd started paying attention to me. I could tell I was turning bright pink and my left leg was shaking, but I couldn't give up now.

"I was embarrassed," I continued. "And I thought as long as no one knew my secrets, I'd be able to get through high school unscathed. But now I realize the opposite is true. You can't create change if you are unwilling to accept reality. If you hold back your whole life, you will never get what you want.

"And so, I want to apologize to all of you, for being dishonest and hiding the truth. There are so many of you that I could have gotten to know better if only I hadn't been so focused on keeping my own secrets." I scanned the crowd and saw Mo standing with Cindy Ramirez. She looked like she was crying, and I suddenly noticed that a few tears had streaked down my own face as well.

I had one thing left to say. "But high school's not over for all of us yet," I announced. "It's not too late for some of us to be honest with ourselves. Someone once said that high school is about broadening your horizons, and at first I didn't understand what that meant, but now I do. It means, this is our chance to reach out and take life by the reins. This is our chance to be the best version of ourselves. It's not too late," I said.

I wiped my wet face and stepped off of the chair as the hushed crowd milled about, stunned by my confession.

And then I did the only thing I could think to do.

I bolted.

Chapter 25

Friday, 2 p.m.

I dashed around the side of the kissing booth and into the gathered crowd. As I did so, I bumped into Mason's shoulder, who had his arm around Bella.

"Lisi?" I heard Bella call after me. But I couldn't look back.

I dodged some girls carrying huge towering piles of purple cotton candy.

I nearly got swatted in the face with the crazy badminton guy, but I kept running. Tears were still streaming down my face.

And then, I ran smack into somebody so hard that I nearly got the wind knocked out of me.

Whoever I'd crashed into was saying "Whoa, whoa, whoa, calm down," and holding me by the shoulders.

I caught my breath, wiped my eyes, and looked up.

It was Johnny.

"Are you okay? What's going on with you?" he asked. His eyebrows were wrinkled up, and he looked concerned.

It was all I could do not to burst into tears as I stared up into Johnny's eyes for a moment, wishing I could explain everything. But no words came. I guess I was all talked out. Plus, I was shaking.

He cleared his throat. And that's when I noticed that he wasn't alone. Some guy — a very *hot* guy with longish black hair and broad shoulders — was standing next to Johnny. He was a bit shorter than Johnny and looked slightly like Diego Luna. I vaguely recognized him but couldn't figure out from where. This guy definitely couldn't be an NHS student.

I looked around and noticed people were staring at us.

"I'm, I'm okay, I just . . ." I had no idea what to say, how to explain myself. "Where were you?" was all I could think to ask.

"I was uh . . . busy," he said. Johnny still had his hands on my shoulders, but now he dropped them and my heart broke a little in that moment. Then his face changed into its usual semi-joking expression. "You miss me that bad?"

I blushed.

"Well, Luc and I were just headed over," Johnny continued, nodding his head toward the guy next to him. "We were just going to grab something from my bag. Will you come with us?" He took hold of my hand.

Wait.

Luc?

Why did that ring a bell?

I didn't exactly want to go *back* to the kissing booth now that I had made such a fool of myself. But I followed Johnny anyway. I didn't want to let go of his hand.

People were whispering all around us.

Jacqueline and Brett were in a big fight, hollering at each other, when we approached, but no one was focused on that. Instead, they all watched as Johnny and Luc and I approached the booth, and Johnny pulled a battery out of his backpack.

He popped the battery into his DVD camera and hit PLAY BACK. "I just wanted to show some things to Mr. Martinez," Johnny explained. He then leaned closer to me and whispered, "This is kind of a big deal."

I stared at him for a second, truly not understanding what was going on. And then Daniel the Dork shouted, "*That's* the celebrity? Luc Martinez?"

And that's when it hit me.

Just as all the girls gathered around the kissing booth started crying, "LUC! LUUUUUC!"

Luc Martinez, the young actor turned film director Johnny was obsessed with, had shown up. And he wasn't there for the kissing booth at all. He was there to see Johnny's work. He'd come all this way just to see Johnny's footage for his mockumentary. He must have gotten one of Johnny's recent mailings.

But Luc *was* a surprise celebrity guest. *Surprise* being the key word!

Uh-oh.

Before Luc knew what was going on, he was being mauled.

"LUUCC!" the girls screamed. There must have been fifty of them, at least. They were pawing at him, puckering at him, begging him to sign his autograph on their textbooks, T-shirts, bare arms.

People began frantically handing tickets to Sarah Singer in order to get a closer look at what was going on at the kissing booth.

Suddenly, the kissing booth was a huge hit. And it was because of Johnny!

Everyone was happy, excited, rowdy, overjoyed.

Everyone, that is, except for Luc Martinez.

I had to do something. I had to rescue the poor guy.

"Come on, I know a way out," I said, grabbing Luc by the hand and gesturing for Johnny to follow.

As the crowd chanted "Luc! Luc! Luc!" we dashed away and I led Johnny and Luc toward the giant movie screen. Quickly, we ducked behind it and caught our breath.

"Lisi!" Johnny hissed. He didn't look happy. "This was my one chance to show Mr. Martinez my work!"

"I know, I know!" I said, frantically looking around, trying to figure out a solution before everyone discovered where we were hidden.

I peered cautiously around the screen and saw the commotion near the kissing booth had only increased. Mrs. Weiss had arrived and was trying to calm everyone down. And then I got an idea.

"Give me your camera!" I cried.

"What? Why?" Johnny asked, holding it protectively.

"Just give it to me!" I commanded. "You can trust me."

Johnny reluctantly put his Minicam in my hands and, before he could protest, I ran back out into the crowd.

I pushed my way through the chanting crowd to Mrs. Weiss.

"Lisi?" She looked at me quizzically as I frantically yanked on her sleeve. "Do you know what all this commotion is about?"

"Yes!" I shouted over the noise of the crowd. "And I need your help! It's an emergency!"

Mrs. Weiss, aka Wise, followed me out of the way. Wise seemed to have a sixth sense for the truth in every situation. Within minutes, she'd helped me organize my plan.

When I came back behind the movie screen, where Johnny was still apologizing to Luc, they both turned to me expectantly.

"Oh God, Lisi, what did you do with my camera?" Johnny asked, seeing that it was not in my hands.

"Johnny, don't freak out. Just trust me."

"What did you do?" he begged, looking like I had stolen his firstborn child.

"Come on," I said. He and Luc followed me back out onto the field.

When we emerged I gestured up to the front of the movie screen.

It suddenly crackled to life.

I looked over to where Mrs. Weiss stood inside the sound booth and she gave me a thumbs-up.

Then Daniel the Dork shouted again and the crowd turned to see what was going on. "Hey!" he yelled, shocked. "That's Brian DeLancy!"

He was pointing at the screen. At the moment, it was focused on a close-up of Brian's face. It was the first scene in Johnny's mockumentary. I had gotten Wise to hook up Johnny's camera to the movie projector.

On the screen, Brian was saying something about Katrina Terrence. "Dude," Brian was saying into the camera. "Kat is the hottest girl in this school." A bunch of people gathering around hooted when they heard that.

Then the film cut to some other kids. Pretty soon, people had stopped squealing at Luc and started paying attention to the movie screen. "Hey, am I on there?" someone called out. Then a few more people started shouting, too. "Who else did you get?" they asked.

"What's on there?" "What did Maya say about me?" "Is Justin on there?" "What did the twins tell you? It isn't true!" and then it got too noisy for me to distinguish anything anymore.

There was a ton of footage, and the rowdiness only increased as more pieces of gossip were revealed in the interviews. But it was pretty cool the way Johnny had done it, splicing back and forth between different quotes, and showing hilarious incidents from school throughout to illustrate each of the quotes. It was all very humorous and subtle and just so *Johnny*.

As I stared up at the screen, two people came and stood at my sides. It was Bella and . . . Mo.

"I want you to know I'm not mad at you anymore. About not telling me. About Brett, I mean," Bella said. Then Mo spoke up. "And I just wanted to tell both of you . . . I'm sorry for acting like a jerk and ditching you guys. I had to get space, I just . . . didn't know how else to handle it." Bella and I nodded solemnly, and I wiped another tear from the corner of my eye. "Also," Mo added, "you should give Jacqueline a chance. She's actually really fun."

Just then, silence descended, and I glanced around.

I noticed even Brett and Jacqueline's arguing had been shushed. Jacqueline's jaw was clamped shut. Because Brett's face had appeared on the movie screen. Apparently it wasn't just me — everyone wanted to know the innermost thoughts of the most popular boy in school.

On the screen, Brett had a huge smirk on his face.

In real life, he looked like a deer caught in headlights.

On the movie screen, Brett was standing in the guys' locker room, twirling a tennis racket. "Nothing stands between me and what I want," he was saying in the film. He shrugged. "Jacqueline? Yeah. That stung. But you know what? She'll regret her decision." He shrugged again and smiled at the camera. "I can definitely find ways of making her jealous. It shouldn't be hard. Any random girl will do."

Just as quickly, the camera spliced away to someone else.

But the damage had been done.

Jacqueline grabbed an ice cream cone out of someone's hand, and before anyone could stop her, she'd nailed Brett (the live one, not the one on the screen) with the ice cream — right in the face. It dripped down onto his American Eagle shirt.

People gasped and laughed and whispered and shouted.

But it wasn't over yet. I couldn't believe how blatantly I'd been duped. I turned and grabbed a jumbo cup of Coke from Celeste.

I marched over and dumped it over Brett's head. "Any random girl will do?" I asked.

The Coke dribbled off his shocked face. He had turned bright red, and stood there opening and closing his mouth, with no words coming out. Finally he turned and ran off the field toward the gym.

Jacqueline went running after him, screaming unintelligibly, though I could make out a lot of high-pitched cursing. A bunch of the Fly Girls ran after her.

As for me, I couldn't look at anyone to see what their faces were saying. I'd had enough humiliation for one day. So I simply sauntered off in the opposite direction and didn't look back.

Chapter 26

Friday, 3p.m.

As I marched into the sun, I felt like I'd grown several inches. I walked tall, crunching discarded napkins and confetti and overly fertilized grass under my feet. I felt surreal. Both happy and sad. Giddy and furious.

I walked by a circle of freshman girls sitting in a ring on the grass by the trees at the edge of the field. Among them were Trish and the friends who'd helped her put up the posters for Jacqueline's booth. When Trish saw me, she shrugged, then held up a Kate Spade notebook. "I didn't mean to be a traitor," she said, smiling. "But Jacqueline offered us these. And free movie tickets. And charm bracelets. All you guys offered us were Milk Duds and your hot Casey Affleck look-alike friend."

I laughed. "Those *are* nice bracelets," I said, seeing

the silver one on Trish's arm sparkle in the sun. And I meant it.

I continued walking. Despite the fact that all of my romantic dreams about Brett had just come crashing down, I felt strangely relieved, like a weight had been lifted. His shallowness hurt, but it was real. I knew the truth. I guess I felt like I deserved it.

And yet part of me was really proud of myself. Because before I'd even *seen* that part of Johnny's film, I'd already made my decision. I hadn't let Brett kiss me. At least, amid the ruins that my life had become, I had done ONE thing right.

And *I* wasn't the one covered in Coke or ice cream.

Feeling spontaneous, I got in line at the Ferris wheel. And then I felt a tap on my shoulder.

It was Johnny.

"Allow me," he said, handing the ticket collector two tickets.

I grinned. We got into a wobbly cart, and the guy operating the machine winked as he pushed the metal safety bar down over our laps.

We were quiet for a while as the rest of the carts filled up. I wasn't sure what to say. And then the wheel actually began to turn.

Agonizingly slowly.

"Hold on to your hats, people!" Johnny shouted, like we were on Splash Mountain instead of the tamest ride in the world.

I laughed. "Somebody stop this thing!" I gasped, pretending to be scared. He chuckled.

Then he stopped chuckling. "It seems like the kissing booth has a good chance of winning the prize," he pointed out. "They were gathering tickets by the boatload when I left. I think Luc actually enjoyed the attention because he sat down and started letting people kiss him!"

"No way!" I laughed. "Who knew it would have worked out so perfectly!"

"So," he began, and then paused, looking out at the trees as our cart got higher. "So why were you running from the kissing booth anyway? I mean, earlier, when you crashed into me like a herd of wild buffalo?"

"Who are you calling a buffalo?" I asked, giggling more. For some reason, being off the ground — or perhaps being through so many emotional ups and downs in one day — was making me punchy.

"Seriously, though, what were you running from?"

I sighed and looked out over the field. "I just, I had to get away. I mean, it was weird."

"Weird?"

"The thing was," I said, "Brett was trying to kiss me. And I just . . . couldn't. I know that's a freakish thing to say, since he's like the most popular guy this side of Mars." I shook my head at myself.

"That *is* weird," Johnny said. "Because I was convinced you wanted nothing more than a kiss from Brett Jacobson."

"What? You knew all along?" I shrieked. And then more quietly I added, "So you thought I liked Brett? Like, *like*-liked him?"

"Well, did you?" His face was unreadable. Maybe it was just the sun making shadows as we made our way around the wheel.

I didn't know how to answer him. Instead, I swiveled a little so I was facing him more. "So is that why you didn't want us to see your DVDs? Because you thought I liked Brett, and you didn't want me to see what he'd said? About how he just wanted to use some random girl to make Jacqueline jealous?" As I said it, I cringed a little, remembering.

"Maybe." Johnny shrugged, squinting into the sun. "Or maybe I just respect the privacy of my subjects."

"Were you mad, then, that I showed your film to the entire school just now?" I asked, worried.

"Well, no. I have to admit, on some level maybe I secretly wanted that to happen," Johnny said, swiveling so he faced me more, too. I breathed a sigh of relief.

"So what I really want to know is, what *other* secrets do you have, Johnny Rothberg?"

"Me? Secrets? What? You're the one with secrets. First you like Brett. Then you don't like Brett. How's a guy supposed to keep up with it all?"

I smiled and shrugged. "I don't know. I guess I just realized, Brett wasn't the one I really wanted to kiss."

Johnny looked at me funny, like I'd just said a math

riddle or something. "So there's some Mystery Dude you would rather make out with?"

"Maybe." I shrugged, feeling myself blushing. But the breeze from the trees and the moving Ferris wheel cooled my face a bit. "What I want to know is, who's the Mystery *Girl* that *you* secretly want to make out with?"

"What?" Johnny asked, raising his eyebrows, his smirk growing into a very amused grin. *Oh great.* So it was true. There *was* some secret mystery girl. And he was obviously enjoying not telling me who it was!

"You have to tell me now!" I practically shouted. Then I realized how loud I was being and brought my voice down. "Seriously, who is Mystery Girl?"

Johnny leaned in closer to me, like he was about to tell me her name. I braced myself for something like Trish, or someone equally as awful. Instead he said, "Tell me who Mystery Dude is first."

I looked at him but couldn't tell what he was thinking. I glanced down and realized we were nearing the top of the Ferris wheel again. I noticed that you could see all of the Spring Carnival from the top of the wheel. Everyone looked so tiny below. So miniscule. Like nothing down on the ground mattered in the grand scheme of things.

Which I suddenly realized was true. I turned back to Johnny.

"Uh-oh," he said, looking serious. "Confession time. Who is the dude? The MD? The Mystery Studmuffin?"

"I think Mystery Boy has zero idea." I smiled at him.

"Really?" Johnny asked. "Another secret, unrequited crush, eh? I'm starting to see an unhealthy pattern here."

"Well, what about Mystery Girl? Does she know?"

Johnny shook his head. "Not a clue." He grinned.

"Hmm," I said, suddenly remembering my fight with Mo. How she'd told me to stop being so oblivious. How she'd been so inexplicably upset with me after she'd found out Johnny didn't like her.

I nudged Johnny. We were right at the top of the wheel now and the cart was swaying slightly.

"Listen," he said. "I'm starting to get confused with all these Mystery People."

"All I'm saying is that maybe Mystery Girl isn't as clueless as everyone thinks. I mean, as *you* think."

"She's not?"

I shook my head dizzily. Now would be a really bad time to faint and then fall to my death. Not when I was this close. Note to self: Next time I'm about to confess my true love for someone, try to do it on solid ground.

"Well, enlighten me, then," Johnny said, looking right into my eyes.

And so I did.

I reached out and put my hands in his luscious, wavy dark hair and brought his face close to mine, and closed my eyes. And then I kissed him.

Johnny's lips were warm and soft. They tasted a little bit like cotton candy and yet also a bit like something else. I felt surrounded by his clean familiar smell, the citrus scent of the shampoo his mom buys for him, mixed with the smell of vintage T-shirts.

And the best part was, he kissed me back. Gently at first, pulling back a little as though each time his lips touched mine, there was a tiny electric shock. Then he wrapped his arms all the way around me and kept kissing me.

It seemed like the wheel had stopped rotating.

Or maybe the entire Ferris wheel had fallen out from under us and we were floating. All I could feel was both of our hearts beating against one another.

I couldn't believe how long I'd wanted this to happen, how foolish I'd been not to realize it sooner. How good he felt in my arms. How fun it was — this whole kissing thing!

When we finally stopped kissing, he grinned at me again.

"So. *Now* will you let me interview you for my film?" he joked.

I blushed. "I still don't think I'd have anything special to add to your movie," I admitted.

"Are you kidding?" he asked.

"What? What's so special about me?" I asked him, dying to know.

"Hah, where to start?" he asked. "Well, first — you are an artist."

I snorted.

"Maybe not famous like your mother, but you're talented," he insisted. "You bring images together just like you bring people together. You're beautiful, smart, and funny." He paused.

He thought I was beautiful! I felt hot all over — in a good way.

Then he leaned in closer to my ear. "But none of those are the reason I like you," Johnny whispered. "I like you because you're . . . Lisi. 'Cause I can't imagine hanging out with anyone else and being happier than I am when I'm with you. Even when you're being *completely* oblivious, you always make me smile."

There was a big grin on his face right now. I love how his face gets when he smiles. It's just so . . . *real*.

Which was why I leaned in and kissed him again.

Of course, aside from just now, I had never been kissed before. But I knew that *this* was the real thing.

TAKE A SNEAK PEEK AT

TOP 8
A novel by Katie Finn

CHAPTER 1

Song: Coming Home/A New Found Glory
Quote: "Many a trip continues long after movement in
time and space have ceased."— John Steinbeck

"We're home!" my mother announced cheerfully as
our SUV passed the town sign: WELCOME TO PUTNAM,
CONNECTICUT. SETTLED 1655. HOME OF THE FIGHTING
PILGRIMS.

We were still twenty minutes away from our house,
but after two weeks away — two weeks away on a *boat* —

I appreciated the sentiment. We had gone on a family trip to the Galápagos Islands, in Ecuador, for spring break.

I'll admit, when my parents first told me where we were going, I had been a little startled. I mean, Ecuador? For spring break? Who spends spring break in *Ecuador*? Besides, I mean, the Ecuadorians. Who live there.

But the islands were amazing — they're completely uninhabited by people, and were made famous when Darwin went down there and discovered the thing about the parrots' beaks that made him realize that evolution, you know, existed.

We'd stayed on a small ship with about twenty other people — including a kind-of cute guy my age — sailing to the islands during the day and exploring them, taking lots of pictures of all the animals, and then going back to the boat to have bad food and sleep.

The animals didn't have any fear, so you could get really close to the penguins, sea lions, and tortoises. All that had been pretty cool.

But.

I'd had to spend the trip in close proximity to my thirteen-year-old Demon Spawn brother, Travis, who at the moment was repeatedly kicking my ankle.

"Thank God we're home," I said, kicking him back, as I stared out the window at the spring flowers bursting into bloom all over the hillsides.

"Didn't you have fun, Madison?" my mother asked as she turned around in the passenger seat to look at me. My father took this opportunity to change the radio station from my mother's financial channel back to the sports report.

"Sean!" my mother said, turning around.

"Laura, I have to hear the scores," my father said. "Travis!" he yelled to my brother, who had not lifted his head from his PSP the entire hour-long ride back from JFK. "Write these down, okay?"

"I can't hear you, Dad," Travis said, obviously lying. Because he had to have heard the question, right?

"Well, I have to hear the stock report," my mother said, reaching to change the station back. "Trav, write down how the Dow did today, okay?"

"*Well*," I said loudly to remind my mother that she had in fact asked me a question, "I thought the Galápagos were nice, but —"

"But she missed her *boyfriend*," Travis singsonged. When both my parents turned around to stare at him — causing the driver in the left lane to swerve suddenly — he seemed to realize that his ruse of being temporarily deafened by his headphones had been foiled. "Crud," he muttered.

"Travis, the Dow —"

"The Braves score —"

"I missed my *friends*," I corrected my brother. But as my parents were back to fighting over the radio and not listening to me, I made a face at him and turned back toward the window. I was counting the minutes until we were home . . . where my laptop and cell, my connections to the outside world, waited.

I hadn't been online in two weeks, and I'd had enough of this involuntary Amish-ness. The only internet connection on the ship was through an ancient computer, and they had charged for internet access. A dollar a minute! And this wouldn't have been that bad, except that it took at least five minutes for the stone-age modem to connect in the first place. And since neither of my parents' BlackBerries had worked, I was SOL in terms of the internet.

The Demon Spawn — no offense to my parents — had surprised me by spending most of his free time in the internet room, angering all the businesspeople who actually had important deals to make, while he was probably just playing fantasy baseball. And since Travis had always hoarded his money like Scrooge, I'd been surprised that he'd been willing to spend so much of it on the World's Slowest Internet.

I might have paid to go online, too, if I hadn't had to buy souvenirs for my friends. But the ones I'd picked out were perfect. I'd gotten a bobble-head Charles Darwin for my best friend, Ruth Miller, a *J'Adore Ecuador!* tote for my Francophile friend Lisa Feldman, and a plush Galápagos bird, the blue-footed booby, for my friend Schuyler Watson.

The present that I'd agonized over the most was for Justin Williamson, my boyfriend of seventeen days (not counting the fourteen days of spring break). I'd finally decided on a pair of carved sea tortoises. I figured we'd each take one, since tortoises mate for life. And I just knew that Justin would understand the implications of this, even though we hadn't yet. Mated, that is. Anyway, I was glad I'd bought the souvenirs rather than spending the $60 it would have taken for me to have checked my e-mail.

As my parents finally reached a truce and turned off the radio, we pulled into our long, winding driveway.

"Finally!" Travis yelled, for once echoing my feelings completely.

"Are you carsick, sweetie?" my mother asked.

"Yeah, Trav," I said. "Is oo sickie?"

"No," he muttered. "Just sick of you."

"Likewise," I said, giving him a shove he totally deserved.

"Mom!" the Demon Spawn yelled.

"Kids!" she said as we pulled into the garage. "I certainly hope you'll be better behaved at dinner tomorrow night."

Which was totally random. Like there was something special about tomorrow night? Like we could behave however we wanted at dinner tonight? But my mother was the CFO of Pilgrim Bank, and so a lot of the time she was just out of it, thinking about how the *baht* was doing, or operating on two hours of sleep because she had to get up at 3 A.M. to deal with the Tokyo markets.

"Sure," I said, getting out of the car, grabbing my purse, and heading toward the house. "No problem."

"And don't forget your suitcase," she called as I headed up the steps to the door, where my father had just finished disabling the alarm.

The suitcase could wait. I had to check my voice mail, my Gmail, my school e-mail, and most important of all, my Friendverse profile.

Friendverse was crucial. Friendverse was the new black, according to Lisa. Everyone I knew had been on it since the beginning of the school year. Before *that*, everyone had been on Facebook, and before that, everyone had been on MySpace. I'd heard rumors that the next site was going to be even better than Friendverse, but since it was called Zyzzx, and nobody knew how to pronounce it, not many people were talking about it yet. But for now, Friendverse was a necessity.

Plus, I knew if I stalled long enough, my father would bring my suitcase up for me. He was the head sportswriter for the *Putnam Post* and spent most of his time at home, writing in his office. I knew the sight of my abandoned suitcase would get to him. He saw the home as his domain — or gridiron, as he called it.

It was only in first grade or something that I realized that most other kids' dads weren't home all day, making them peanut-butter-and-banana sandwiches and telling them all about the '34 Giants lineup.

Which was too bad for them, in my opinion. My dad made — and still makes — a mean PB&B.

"Madison, suitcase!" my father yelled at me as I stepped inside, my mother behind me. I heard the phone ring, and my mother hurried to answer it.

"Later, okay?" I said, one foot on the stairs. I had a profile to check!

My father shook his head. "I'll help you carry it, Madison, but I'm not doing it for you."

Damn. That had been my plan.

"And I'd recommend now," he said. "Unless you want your brother going through it . . . again."

That was all I needed to hear. After last year's trip to Spain, I'd left my suitcase in the hall for a little bit — okay, two weeks. But whatever, it had been heavy. And I was just taking out what I needed, to lighten it up enough to carry it upstairs to my room. That was when Travis went through it, stole my bra, and used it in his seventh grade art project, "Ground Control to Major Travis," as the base for the space station or whatever it was supposed to be. And his art teacher hadn't realized that there was a *bra* in his student's project — a stolen bra, at that — and it had gone onto a state festival and won third place.

And of course all of Travis's friends knew that it was my (admittedly somewhat padded) bra that was currently on display in Putnam Middle School's trophy case. This had made me particularly popular whenever I had to pick Travis up after school.

I grabbed my suitcase by the top, and my dad picked up the bottom. I could hear my mom continuing to talk animatedly on the phone in the kitchen, with the low buzz of the stock report in the background.

"Oof," my father said, stumbling under the suitcase's weight. "What's in here? You know we weren't supposed to bring any rocks out of the country."

"Just souvenirs and stuff," I said as we hauled it up, stair by stair.

"Can you believe your mother?" my dad asked as we paused to take a breather. "We just left these people, and she wants to have dinner with them tomorrow night?"

"Yeah," I agreed absently. My thoughts were on my laptop, and how long it would be before I could have my hands on it again.

"I mean, is it too much to ask that we stop hanging out with these people and listening to their interminable golfing stories?"

I had no idea what my dad was talking about, but I really didn't care. The sooner we got the suitcase up to my room, the sooner I could go online, turn my cell on, and reconnect with the outside world again.

"There," my dad said, dragging the suitcase the last few feet, dropping it onto my carpet, and clutching his back. "That probably made my chiropractor very rich."

"Oh," Travis said, appearing in my doorway, looking disappointed. "I didn't realize you would have brought your suitcase up already. I wanted to, um, help."

"Out!" I yelled at him.

"Don't yell at your brother," my dad said absently, doing back-stretching exercises and therefore missing the incredibly rude gesture Travis made at me as he left. Like I was supposed to *let* him continue to use my lingerie in his art projects? Um, no. I don't think so.

As my father hobbled off in search of a heating pad, I closed the door behind him, looked around and smiled. I was home.

It had taken about three years, but I'd finally gotten my room the way I wanted it. This was after many arguments with my mother, who kept wanting her decorator to "do something in neutrals." But I'd prevailed, and now it was perfect. Pink and green, with one whole wall in cork, making it into a huge bulletin board. The room was a little messy, but I could always find what I needed, so I really didn't understand what Gabby, who cleaned for us, was always complaining about.

On my desk were stacks of college catalogs — my mother was pushing for Vassar, and my dad wanted me to go to Michigan, but I had a feeling only because he wanted good seats to home games — and my piles of unfinished homework.

There were also towering stacks of paperback mysteries — Agatha Christie, Sherlock Holmes, John D. MacDonald, Dashiell Hammett. My English teacher, Mr. Underwood, had been assigning them all semester, and to my surprise, I'd really gotten into them.

My walls were covered with posters from the productions I'd been in at Putnam High School. There were the normal ones: *The Seagull* (sophomore year, my first lead. I'd gotten the part of Nina after a grueling audition process against Sarah Donner; she'd ended up understudying me), *Wait Until Dark* (last winter, I'd beaten out Sarah for Susy, the lead. Things had gone so disastrously during the last performance that I tried not to think about it too much), *Noises Off!* (this past fall; I'd lost out on Belinda, the part I really wanted, to Sarah, and had ended up playing Brooke, who spends most of the play in her underwear), and *Romeo and Juliet* (sophomore year winter; I'd played Juliet, Sarah had understudied).

Then there were the posters for the yearly musical, which was always an original adaptation: freshman year's *Frankly, Anne . . . The Musical Diary of Anne Frank* and last year's *Willy! Death of a Musical Salesman*. As I spotted my script of this year's production — *Great Dane: The Musical Tragedy of Hamlet* — lying on my bed, I felt suddenly guilty that I'd forgotten to bring it on the trip with me. We were supposed to be off-book when we came back, and I knew that Sarah — who was understudying me again — would be such a pain to deal with if I went up on a line.

My bulletin-wall was covered with pictures of me and my friends: Ruth and me in third grade (the year I moved to Putnam from Boston and we became best friends), then Ruth and I dressed up at this year's Winter Dance. There were pics of me, Schuyler, and Ruth looking bored at the French Appreciation lecture that Lisa had dragged us to last month; Shy and Ruth wearing their MAD FOR MAD FOR SECRETARY buttons from last month's election; Lisa and her boyfriend, Dave Gold, making faces at the camera; the class couple, Jimmy Arnett and Liz Franklin, with their arms around each other (as usual); a series of increasingly crooked shots from my lab partner Brian McMahon's last party; and the front page of the *Putnam Pilgrim* that showed the results of the ridiculous recount that Connor Atkins had demanded when I beat him — twice — for senior class secretary.

On my bedside table, there was a stack of newly developed pictures, the ones taken at the Spring Carnival just before I'd left, all of me and Justin, looking so cute together. And sure, in a lot of the pictures, Justin seemed to be blinking or looking the wrong way, but I didn't care. He still looked completely adorable.

I grabbed my cell from where I'd left it on the bed and turned it on, desperate to call Justin, only to see that the red battery icon was illuminated, and the phone refused to turn on. I groaned, remembering the reason I hadn't brought it with me — in addition to the fact I only would have been able to use it on the rides to and from the airport — I'd forgotten to charge it. I plugged it into my charger and flopped down on my bed.

I pushed aside the pile of clothes I'd rejected during my last-minute packing frenzy, and fired up my laptop. I typed in my password — **madmacdonaldsmac** —

gently, as my computer had been acting up a lot just before the trip.

Frank Dell — or Dell, as he preferred to be called. I believe the first time I met him, his actual phrasing was, "I'm Frank Dell. Hold the Frank." Which just sounds weird, if you ask me — had fixed it for me just before the trip. He was the school's resident computer expert, who fixed problem laptops much more cheaply than The Computer Store in town.

And repairing my laptop had apparently become my responsibility ever since I had it customized and painted pink. My mother hadn't been too happy about this; convinced that the paint had somehow damaged the computer, she told me I was on my own with repairs. Travis had offered to loan me the money — at a 21% interest rate — but I preferred to take my chances with Dell. But since he had just gotten it working again, mostly — I still couldn't type the letter Q — I didn't want to make any sudden movements or do anything that might scare it back into the Blue Screen of Death.

I logged onto the internet and pulled up Friendverse. I knew exactly what I was going to see: my page, which I'd just redone before I left, with a really cute striped background; all my information; and my Top 8, ranked in order of importance — Justin, Ruth, Lisa, Schuyler, Dave, Jimmy and Liz, Sarah Donner, and Connor Atkins. I'd actually only put Connor there because it looked good during the campaign, and Sarah there to try and ease tensions between us after the cast list had been posted. But I figured that it had been long enough in both cases, and I made a mental note to move them out.

I couldn't wait to see all my profile views, the new comments I'd gotten, recent buddy invites, and what had been going on on my friends' profiles. I typed in my Friendverse password, which was the same as my regular password plus an exclamation point, and waited to log on.

I stretched and looked around my room, glad to be home. I smiled as I looked at all the pictures of my friends. Life was good.

My login had gone through, so I clicked on my Friendverse profile.

And screamed.

To Do List:
Read all the Point books!

♡ 📖 ♡

Airhead
By **Meg Cabot**

Suite Scarlett
By **Maureen Johnson**

The Year My Sister Got Lucky
South Beach
French Kiss
Hollywood Hills
By **Aimee Friedman**

The Heartbreakers
The Crushes
By **Pamela Wells**

*This Book Isn't Fat,
It's Fabulous*
By **Nina Beck**

Wherever Nina Lies
By **Lynn Weingarten**

Summer Boys
By Hailey Abbott
Summer Boys
Next Summer
After Summer
Last Summer

In or Out
By Claudia Gabel
In or Out
Loves Me, Loves Me Not
Sweet and Vicious
*Friends Close,
Enemies Closer*

Hotlanta
By Denene Millner
and Mitzi Miller
Hotlanta
If Only You Knew
What Goes Around